ARCHANGEL

Fire From Heaven - Book 2

AVA MARTELL

Copyright © 2018 by Ava Martell

All rights reserved.

Photo by Roman Stetsyk / Shutterstock.com

No part of this book may be reproduced in any form or by any electronic or mechanical means, including information storage and retrieval systems, without written permission from the author, except for the use of brief quotations in a book review.

❦ Created with Vellum

Sign up for Ava Martell's newsletter to receive updates on new releases as well as free sneak previews of what's coming next in the Fire From Heaven series.

Follow Ava on social media

Facebook
Twitter
Tumblr
Instagram

For those left behind

1

ELISSA

The first step is always the hardest.

Your hands tremble as they shove whatever items are important enough to spare a few precious seconds on into a suitcase, but when you slam the lid closed they're steady. You've been scared long enough.

You tried to do things the right way. Tried to go to the police. Filled out meaningless reports that ended up being nothing more than tinder for the wildfire of his rage.

You tried, and you weren't the one that failed.

Sometimes you show up at our door alone, on foot with nothing but the clothes on your back and maybe a purse you snatched up as you ran out the door. Other times you're clutching a cat carrier or a leash because you know anything small and helpless left behind will end up dead. And more often than either of us like to think of you're clasping the fingers of a hollow-eyed child, their thousand-yard stare mirroring your own.

You hide the mottled bruises under long sleeves and thick foundation until they fade to a sickly yellow-green and disappear, and for the first time you aren't waiting for them to inevitably be replaced with more. Some small part of you can even imagine being able to hear a raised voice without flinching one day.

You're afraid, and you're angry.

But you're finally in the right place.

There's no sign on our door. We've never posted an ad in the yellow pages, even back in the days when phonebooks actually made it inside the house instead of the quick trip from the mailbox to the recycling bin. We don't have a slick website splashing our services across the internet.

But you still find us.

Our names slip from hand to hand, whispered like a password or prayer in clinics and shelters by social workers and nurses that have seen too much. A few of you even hear about us from the police, cops disgusted with a system that hamstrings them until someone ends up dead. They scrawl out our number on a coffee-stained napkin and crush it into the palm of those who need it most.

We're the last stop for most of you, and we know it. We remember every name and every history.

Today, your name is Tara. You tell your story in halting words, your soft voice thick with tears you're still too afraid to let fall. You ran away to New Orleans from a dusty town in the Florida panhandle, hoping for bright lights and new beginnings in the big city.

But like a curse dogging your heels, he followed. And he found you.

Caila presses a streaming mug of tea into your hands, and you drink the hot liquid mechanically. She smiles, and you look up at her like she's your own personal angel, saving you with a cup of too-hot chamomile tea.

The look you give me a moment later, your eyes locking with mine as the hot tea scalds your tongue, is different.

Because no woman walks through our door without knowing just what she's asking for.

Caila smiles at you, that pure, serene look of peace, and I can already feel the shackles around your soul starting to loosen from a few minutes in her presence.

If the rest of the Heavenly host had been more like Caila, I might have made a different decision all those years ago.

You look at Caila and see what she is. It radiates out of her like light, so beautiful and blinding that even a jaded Hell-bound bitch like myself gets dazzled by it. She's here to heal you, to help you stitch together your tattered psyche so that you can come out the other side whole.

And me?

I'm the last thing they see.

A hundred lifetimes ago, the girl I once was might have hesitated. Might have tried to forgive. Not anymore. Tara meets my eyes over the smooth ceramic of the mug, and buried under years of fear and impotent rage at the hand life dealt her I can see the smoldering embers of her spirit starting to catch.

I don't make the choice for any of you. You've had every decision ripped from you, and I refuse to add to it. I couch it in words like "disappear" and "untraceable" and soothing phrases like "he'll never hurt anyone again," but despite the ugly words thrown in your faces for years, none of you are stupid.

You know tonight will start with broken fingers and end with blood.

When I have them on their knees, staring up at me as they cradle the ruined hands they once used to torment, I always give them time to beg.

Some do. Some swear that they'll quit drinking, get counseling, find God, anything they think might appeal to my fragile female heart. They keep up the act until I curve my lips around the single syllable that they never listened to.

"No."

They hear that one word, and that look of desperate repentance always twists into the same cold hatred as they lash out at me.

Or they try to.

I'm just a girl, after all. Another weak, breakable creature they can bring to heel like a wayward dog.

Except I stopped being just a girl long ago.

The woman they tortured is being cared for by an angel, but they get to feel a taste of Hell's wrath before I send them down to Lucifer's kingdom.

I take my time.

After all, they never made it easy on you.

Breaking bones sounds a bit like making popcorn. Except popcorn doesn't scream.

Later, I wash the blood from underneath my fingernails, watching as the last trace of their existence slides down the drain in a thin red stream.

I don't crouch in a shower, sobbing in horror at taking a life, however vile and cruel that life might have been. I don't stare at my fingers, remembering the sensation of his heartbeat stuttering and finally failing. I don't regret.

After all, I wasn't the one who made this choice.

He did, the moment he raised his hand to you that first time.

I open the door and walk out into the night air, the humidity sticky on my skin. When the body is found, it'll be labeled as a home invasion gone wrong. The overworked police will make a cursory investigation, searching for the murderous man that committed this crime. They never think to search for a women.

Soon enough, his name is forgotten, pushed into a cold case file as the city moves on.

We'll never see you again. What we do survives by secrecy and silence, but we know you'll keep close watch on the news. When you get that knock on your door, and the uniformed officer delicately breaks the news that you're now a widow, you shed your last tears for him. Only these tear tracks aren't from fear. As you sob into the officer's chest, you wait to feel remorse that never comes.

You're free. You're finally free.

And in your heart you vow to never let yourself be chained again.

"How'd it go?"

Caila always waits up for me these nights, perched on the edge of the heavy oak desk that dominates the back wall, ignoring whatever soft furniture she filled the living room turned office with in an attempt to make the space feel inviting.

I shrug, tossing my bag onto the cobalt velvet of the sofa before dropping down to the soft cushions myself. These nights always leave me drained.

Just because something isn't hard doesn't mean it's easy.

"The usual," I reply, rolling my shoulder and wincing at the tightness in my neck. I need a drink or three, a shower, and about twelve hours of sleep, but instead I turn my attention to the fretting angel watching me from a few feet away.

"You know I worry about you." The soft concern in Caila's voice has me instantly regretting my flippant tone, and I sit up straighter, peeling my eyes open and resisting the urge to sink deeper into the cushions.

I pull my lips into a thin approximation of a smile as Caila scrutinizes me, her grey-blue eyes lingering on my own just long enough to assure herself that I'm as whole and unharmed as I ever am.

"No complications?" she asks, pushing herself off the edge of the desk and making her way over to the tiny kitchen. My eyes slip shut again as I hear her bustling in the kitchen, and a moment later I feel the smooth wineglass pressed into my hand. The pine scent of the Retsina hits my nose and I smile as I take a sip, the sharp taste comforting in centuries of familiarity. I open my eyes just in time to see Caila's nose wrinkling with disgust at my choice of beverage.

"I still don't know how you can drink that." She shudders as I take an exaggerated gulp for her benefit. "It tastes like something you should clean your floors with."

"Philistine." I heave myself off of the sofa. I can already feel the balm of Caila's presence smoothing down the sharp edges of rage that tonight's encounter awakened. "How's Tara?"

Caila brightens, and I know what happened before she speaks. It radiates off her like sunlight as she flits around the room, pouring herself a glass of red wine and settling back into the overstuffed armchair across from me. Now that I'm safely home, and she's satisfied that she won't need to end her night wreaking Heavenly justice on a sinful human, the stiff formality that she can never quite shake drains away. Caila kicks off her shoes, the dainty blue heels clattering on the scuffed wooden floors as she swings her long legs over the arm of the chair.

"She'll be fine," Caila says, gesturing to the unassuming book sitting open on the desk. I don't have to look to know that tonight's page will have Tara's name and story written in Caila's neat hand, the Enochian text hiding the book's contents from prying eyes. "She's staying in New Orleans. She was rebuilding her life before he showed up. I can't blame her for not wanting to uproot herself again."

I nod, half-listening to Caila as she talks about putting Tara in contact with a church out in Metairie with a domestic violence support group. She knows that my attention isn't focused on her, but Caila keeps talking anyway, her low voice the same reassuring chatter that calms everyone that crosses our threshold.

Nights like this bring out the reflective nature I bury so successfully in the daylight hours. I sip my wine without comment, letting the bitter taste wash over my tongue as my eyes slowly survey the room.

Beyond the décor changes that Caila insists on at each new location, it's the same as a dozen other offices we've set up across the country over the years. The unassuming shotgun house sits on the edge of Mid-City where the bright lights of the French Quarter fade. Here on Iberville Street, most are just trying to scratch out a living and no one gives our late night and early morning visitors a second glance.

It's a long way from Phoenicia.

The thick taste of pine resin clings to my tongue, and I can almost smell the twin scents of saltwater and decaying shellfish that rode the ocean breezes whipping through my childhood back in Sidon.

I blink my eyes, shaking my head to push out the unwanted memory, and I notice that Caila's voice has trailed off into silence.

"You're not fine."

"I'm just tired," I counter, brushing off Caila's well-meaning concern. "We all aren't angels, Caila. I'm still human enough that I need sleep on occasion. I promise, I'm fine," I repeat.

Caila looks unconvinced, but she holds her tongue as I disappear down the narrow hallway.

The old pipes creak when I turn the shower on, but the steam rises quickly, billowing clouds filling the room with clammy heat. I leave my clothes in a heap on the floor, the utilitarian black fabric stark against the pristine white tile.

The water is just a few degrees short of unpleasant, but I leave the temperature alone, ducking my head under the stream and breathing in the humid air as my dark hair hangs in a soggy curtain around my face.

I blink water out of my eyes, and hurry through washing my hair, letting the memory of tonight slide off my skin and through the drain at my feet.

"You're a pretty one. You don't see eyes like that every day."

They always say something about my eyes.

I twist the knob with more force than is necessary and hear the metal creak. I yank my hand back, knowing that Caila's belief in my healthy mental state will deteriorate pretty fast if I destroy the bathroom after a routine job.

I swipe my palm across the mirror, clearing a swath of steam away.

My eyes stare back at me, pale blue as an Artic spring and just as cold.

And not for the first time, I wonder what he'd think of me now.

2
MICHAEL

Heaven is burning.

Not literally, of course, but I suspect even an inferno engulfing the very gates wouldn't have my brothers and sisters in this much of a frenzy.

"The human needs to be destroyed."

"Do you wish to end up like Uriel?"

"She made her choice. She chose Hell and him."

A dozen voices clamor over each other, arguing over the fate of a human they've never met, and I bite back the urge to scoff at their anger at her "choice."

Choice. There's that word again.

Did she really have a choice at all? Uriel slaughtered his way through her family line for centuries. Heaven tore apart her young life, and for all his innumerable faults, Lucifer was kind to her.

Lucifer loved her.

I never imagined I'd see the day when my errant brother would risk his skin for anything but his own pride, but I saw Lucifer stand before Uriel's blade with my own eyes, ready and willing to trade his life to spare Grace.

In the aftermath, bloody and battered, surrounded by the rubble of the hotel bar, they still only had eyes for each other. I watched Lucifer twist one of her blonde curls around his finger, a touch that spoke of familiarity and affection, not the base lust I'd grown to expect from him. That small, intimate gesture showed me how Lucifer had changed far more than any grand declaration ever could.

It wasn't the first time I'd felt envy burn through me like a sickness concerning my brother, but the depth of the emotion still had me reeling.

He defied our Father, shattered every rule, and somehow still won.

And I, the ever-obedient son, was left to collect Uriel's body and return to Heaven alone.

"Enough!"

Raphael's voice cuts through the din, silencing the squabbles of the Thrones and Dominions as they weigh the pros and cons of starting yet another war without pausing to consider the cost.

To them, she's just another human, no more important than any other. To Lucifer, she's everything, and no part of me doubts that my brother will rip through the gates and tear a bloody swath through Heaven if any harm comes to her.

In those moments, I find myself understanding Uriel far more than I ever expected to, and I slip away to the sound of Raphael chastising the crowd.

It won't work.

Once we all would have fallen in line at the first order. In those days, Lucifer's infraction was so unheard of, so utterly inconceivable that a thousand years passed without another hint of insurrection from anyone. Lucifer's war left scars on all our memories, and we followed Father's orders like good little soldiers, never questioning if what we did was right.

Myself especially.

The voices of my brethren fade as I follow the familiar path to Eden. Without Uriel's hulking form standing sentry by the gates, the garden seems subdued.

Then I step inside and the word subdued drops from my mind. However the humans might imagine it, Eden is no manicured garden with neat rows of flowers swaying in the breeze. The plants grow wild, tendrils of jasmine twisting and twining through rosebushes, tall irises standing stately above tangles of wildflowers, the tiny white bells of the lilies of the valley poking through the ground cover. The overlapping scents of a hundred blooms make the air feel thick as honey, and for all his madness, I can't blame Uriel for retreating here.

Respite from the back-biting and endless politics the other angels constantly embroil themselves in feels like a balm. I've scarcely been back for a week, and all I can do is wonder how I never saw it before. Was I so caught up in my perpetual obedience that I missed what Heaven has become?

A tiny, poisonous thought has already started to take root in my mind, and no amount of hiding in Eden can stamp it out.

Lucifer was right.

I hear the crunch of the sand and gravel and turn around, schooling my features into the serene visage of someone who isn't discovering a sudden empathy with the Fallen One.

Raphael regards me coolly. "You left." His voice is flat, but free of accusation. If any part of him notices the turmoil running riot in me, he doesn't mention it. Raphael takes a step closer and rests his arm on my shoulder, his head cocked to the side as he scrutinizes me.

I doubt he even realizes what he's doing. The perpetual healer, taking stock of the physical and mental state of those around him is as unconscious as breathing for Raphael.

A head shorter than both Uriel and myself, there's no

mistaking Raphael for a warrior. Like all the Archangels, his hands are no strangers to wielding a blade, but he was a healer first, always preferring to use his talents to mending rifts in flesh and soul rather than causing them.

Another spark of envy flares in me, and I hate myself a bit more in the face of my brother's concern.

"You can't stay, Michael."

I open my mouth to protest, but close it just as quickly. I failed in my mission, after all. It didn't matter that there was no stopping Uriel without ending his life. One of my brothers still died under my watch at the hands of a human.

I just never expected Raphael to start handing out sentences.

Raphael sighs, shaking his head slightly at whatever he sees written on my face. He squeezes my shoulder briefly before stepping back. "I don't want to ask this of you again, Michael, but you need to return. You heard them." He cuts his eyes back to the gate, and I'm startled at how weary he looks.

"I hope I was able to make them see reason, but so many of them can't see anything but how Lucifer had a hand in this, even if it wasn't his hand that slew Uriel." Raphael scrubs his hand over his eyes, the gesture shockingly human. "If one of them chooses to take punishment into their own hands and harms the human. . ." Raphael's voice trails off, and his warm brown eyes glimmer with curiosity at his next words. "Is it really true, brother? What they say about Lucifer and this mortal?"

I exhale slowly as I try to gather my thoughts into some semblance of order before nodding slowly, chuckling at the look of utter astonishment on Raphael's face. "If I hadn't seen it myself, I wouldn't believe it either. He's different, Raphael." I quickly sober as I add, "But in some ways, very much the same. If the Last is harmed, and Lucifer even suspects Heaven had a hand in it. . . I think the first war will pale."

Raphael can't hide the flash of alarm across his face which quickly fades into resolution. "You agree then? That someone needs to keep an eye on the both of them until this blows over?"

I nod numbly, barely listening to Raphael's words even though the last thing I want is to return to Earth so soon. I have no intention of making Lucifer aware of my presence, but I can't help mulling over his and Uriel's words.

"You did have your little detour in Phoenicia all those years ago, didn't you?"

"We all remember your little sabbatical in Phoenicia with your blasphemous little whore."

"And how is dear Elissa? Tell me, does she still despise you?"

I pick at the words like a half-healed wound as Raphael takes his leave and I'm alone in the garden once more.

Lucifer was always a master at knowing just which words would cut the deepest. Uriel wielded his words like a cudgel - no finesse or subtlety, but I still ended up bloody by the end as they both brought up the memories of her I've been trying to bury for centuries.

Elissa.

I whisper it, my voice sounding impossibly loud in the still air of the garden. It's the first time I've let my lips form her name in centuries, since I shuttered myself against the memory of what I lost.

What I was forced to give up.

Lucifer's words sliced open the scars with surgical precision, and I can't stop myself from poking the wound.

Elissa.

A beautiful mistake. A mistake that cost us both, but her most of all.

God's Poison.

God's Blade.

God's Bloody Fists.

I was content with just being that until she showed me another choice.

And how did you repay her, Michael? By sending her straight to me.

I shake my head, trying to clear it and force the image of her back into my memory.

She's long gone. It's been centuries since I sought her out, watching her like a voyeur on the streets of Paris, swallowed in petticoats and yards of pale lace. With her dark hair hidden under a powdered wig, her ice blue eyes were even more striking as they stared into the darkness where I hid.

It was a long way from Phoenicia and the cliffs of Sidon where I met her, and she was many years removed from being that girl.

She took a step forward, and her hand twitched, ready to conjure a light and reveal my hiding place.

Like a coward, I flew, and the ball of flame cupped in her palm illuminated nothing but an empty alley.

I haven't looked for her since.

I made my choice, all those years ago, and she's right to hate me for it.

Elissa never was the forgiving type.

The honeyed air of Eden has gone cloying to my senses, and I choke on the heavy scent. The beauty of this place feels like a cage.

Once more the dutiful soldier, I shoulder my duty and walk out of the garden, mentally preparing myself for the messy, chaotic world that waits outside.

If she could see me now, see the doubt seeping into my veins, I think she'd laugh.

Too little, too late to save us. To save her.

I spread my wings and go.

3
ELISSA

I notice the cracked glass first.

Thin as spider silk, the cracks crisscross the heavy glass panes inset into the rust-colored front door. From a few steps back, the fissures make the glass appear frosted, but when I step closer the hairline cracks that turn the clear windows opaque and fuzzy become obvious.

The thick bars of the security door are still intact, but the metal of the lock is warped like paper curled in a flame. I slide my finger through the opening and pull, the distorted lock popping out easily as the door creaks open.

I turn the doorknob slowly, unsurprised that the shattered knob turns freely. The slight movement as I push the door inward is enough to shake the glass loose, and pebbles of safety glass rain down at my feet.

My hand slides to my hip as I step over the threshold, my boots crunching on the glass underfoot. The smooth hilt of the Hell-forged dagger tucked into my belt fits perfectly into my palm as the door swings open and I scan the ruins of my current address.

I've never been terribly sentimental, and even if I was the

type to cry over broken dishes and torn fabric, a few months in a dwelling isn't enough to make it a home. But I still freeze in the doorway, anger surging through me at the damage in front of me.

I kick the door closed behind me, the last shards of glass still clinging to the window frame clinking on the scarred wood floors. Whoever did this is long gone, and the noise of the slamming door is the only outlet I have for my fury.

The blue velvet couch and the overstuffed chairs that dominate the small room are upended, the fabric ripped open. Springs and stuffing poke through the wounds in the cushions, spilling out like entrails. Feathers from one of the shredded pillows litter the floor like blackened snow. The scent of scorched fabric and burnt feathers hangs in the air, acrid and heavy.

The desk is still upright, but the thick oak top is cracked down the middle, and the lacquer covering the surface is bubbled and charred from heat.

Not that I'd ever thought otherwise, but whoever did this certainly wasn't human.

"Caila?" I call, expecting no answer.

The small kitchen is as much of a wreck as the rest of the house. I step over the remnants of a crushed bottle, the red wine it held drying into a sticky puddle that looks far too much like congealed blood. More broken dishes litter the floor, and the cabinet that held them gapes open, the door barely clinging to one broken hinge. I run my finger over the smear on the dark wood, and it comes away tacky and red.

And this isn't wine.

I hear something pop under my boot, and I rock back on my heels to stare at the crushed teacup on the floor. Caila had shown up with the ridiculous tea set the day after we moved in. Delicate as butterfly wings, something about the fussy little cups captivated her, and she lined them up on a shelf above the unused stove like candy colored soldiers.

Now it's nothing more than ruined bits of mint green porcelain ground into the cracks between the floorboards.

Next to it is another feather, but this one isn't another curled piece of white fluff from a pillow. Long as my forearm and tawny gold as an eagle's, the edge of the feather is mussed and bent. I crouch down and pluck it from the ground, clenching my hand around it and feeling the faint whisper of Caila's presence.

She didn't go easy.

I've seen enough.

I back out of the kitchen, and stride down the narrow hallway to the bedroom I claimed as my own, the feather still clutched in my hand. Spartan and spare, this room began as little more than a place to sleep, something Caila with her constant desire to nest chides me on in every new location.

"You humans make such interesting things!" she would say, sidling into my room with a rug or lamp in one of her deceptively fragile hands. "What's the point of living forever if it's in an empty room?"

I always give in, and as time passes my monk-like quarters begin to resemble a room an actual person lives in.

It amuses me more than it likely should that a celestial being does a better job at feigning normal humanity than I do.

Tonight though, I don't notice the decorations. I don't glance at the large painting of the stormy ocean Caila hung on my back wall. The mesmerizing swirls of blues and greens and blacks fail to captivate me. My eyes are on one thing only, the heavy trunk resting on the floor below it.

I drop to my knees, running my hand over the lock and sighing with relief when I feel the faint tingle of magic that tells me it hasn't been tampered with. I lean forward, my lips barely an inch from the lock and whisper "Open." Obediently the lock pops, and I flip open the trunk, staring in at two thousand years of history and knowledge and power contained in a few square feet of oak and metal.

Wrapped in a length of roughly woven linen is the object I want. I unwind the fabric quickly and run my fingers over the hammered bronze bowl, the sharp angles of the Phoenician text etched deeply into the metal. "See what is hidden," I murmur.

I duck back into the hallway, the damage to the house not even registering as I fling open the cabinets, searching for an unbroken bottle of wine. I see one leaning precariously against the fridge, the neck cracked but mostly intact. Popping the cork splits the glass even more, but it doesn't matter.

Not for what I have planned.

I pour the bottle into the bowl, the deep crimson looking like blood as it fills the bronze vessel. I shove my sleeve up, baring my forearm, and draw the razor-honed edge of my dagger across it. Blood wells up from the cut, and I hang my arm over the bowl, watching as it drips into the wine.

The cut heals quickly, and I dip the feather into the mixture, the tawny gold of Caila's feather disappearing under the thick ruby liquid. I hover my palm over the smooth surface and concentrate, feeling the mixture bubble and then ignite, a plume of black smoke rising from the bowl.

"Show me," I hiss, staring into the flame, waiting for the shifting smoke to coalesce into an image or a clue, anything to tell me where Caila is.

The smoke drifts upward, and I repeat myself, the words coming out as a snarl instead of a beseeching request. I learned long ago, magic is a wild dog. Show it fear or weakness, and it'll tear out your throat.

I'm not asking for Caila's location. I'm demanding it.

The smoke swirls as my power wars with whatever's blocking me. I push harder, feeling the muscles in my arms tighten as though preparing for attack. I taste the tang of iron on the smoke, and the half-healed cut on my forearm burns.

"Show me!" I yell for a third time, my voice rising above the roaring in my ears. The smoke thickens, the flames rising above the side of the bowl, consuming the contents, and some idle part of my mind is grateful that I disconnected the smoke detector the day we moved in.

The smoke rises higher, crawling along the ceiling like a living creature, and I feel pressure around my throat like fingers digging into my windpipe. I see a flicker of something in the smoke – heavy iron chain and a deceptively normal door - before the fire eats through the last of its fuel and abruptly goes out.

I gasp, sitting back on my heels and frantically drawing oxygen into my choked lungs as the smoke dissipates around me, leaving nothing more than a haze in the air.

Resting in the now empty bowl is the feather from Caila's wing, still untouched by the flames.

Whoever has Caila was able to match an angel in battle and has enough power to ward her location from me.

It's time to bring in the big guns.

And I know just who to call.

I EXPECTED her to be taller.

The supernatural world loves its gossip as much as much as any human, and the Last siding with Hell hasn't escaped the attention of any witch, medium or demon this side of the Mississippi. But it's the rumors that Lucifer has fallen in love that shock me far more than the idea of someone choosing the Pit over Heaven.

When they show up, I'm sitting behind the desk, my feet up on the ruined surface as I toss the rough iron coin etched with Lucifer's sigil into the air. He chuckles as I palm the coin and get to my feet, his face breaking into a wide grin at the sight of me.

"Elissa, it's been too long."

"Far too long," I agree, glancing around him at the diminutive blonde hovering a few feet back. "And this must be the girl who domesticated the Devil."

Grace tries and fails miserably to stifle her laughter at that.

"He's hardly what I'd call domesticated," she says, stepping around Lucifer to stand in front of me. I've always been tall for a woman, especially in the time of my birth, and Grace is a full head shorter than me, but the power radiating off her makes it easy to forget her small stature.

I can already see why she enthralls Lucifer. She moves like an immortal, sure and steady with a confidence rolling off her that has little to do with Lucifer at her side. She fought for him, but she fought for herself first, and it shows.

I like her already.

Lucifer's eyes track her every movement with a possessive protectiveness I've never seen from him. If the dirt Caila relayed to me in the aftermath of the city going mad is true, Uriel nearly killed them both, and Lucifer looks like he's still waiting for Heavenly retaliation to strike.

He knows his family far too well to trust in the calm after the storm.

My curiosity can wait though. Caila can't. "As much as I've been dying to meet you, this isn't a social call." The crashing reality of my friend's absence hits me, and I lean back against the desk, looking up at Lucifer with a desperation I haven't shown anyone since I was a barefoot girl begging at a witch's door. "I need your help, Lucifer."

"Does it have anything to do with the state this room is in?" Lucifer asks.

I nod. "I came back to it like this. I was only gone for a few hours. Caila put up a fight, obviously."

"Caila," Lucifer repeats slowly, and in the space of a second I see his hackles rise. "She's one of Uriel's, isn't she?" It isn't a question.

"Was," I reply. "Hasn't been for a long time." Lucifer takes a step forward, putting himself between me and Grace, and I'm shaken at the naked display in front of me. This isn't the Lucifer I knew who was the most concerned with spitting on Heaven whenever he was offered the chance.

This is a man who, for the first time in thousands of years, has something to lose.

Even with all of our history, bringing up the name of an angel to him, especially one tied so closely to Uriel, is a risk.

But I've never been one to take the easy way.

"You of all people know the political bullshit in Heaven. Uriel had a lot more support than anyone knew." I hold Lucifer's gaze, his cold, dark eyes searching mine for any hint of treachery. History or not, I have no doubt that he would end me if he thought I was working for Uriel, and I have to fight the urge to snort in derision at the thought of that.

Lucifer's new girl isn't the only one who lost everything because of Heaven.

"She wasn't helping him," I repeat. "Anyone that disagreed with Uriel's methods did what they could in the background, but even most of his detractors weren't willing to risk their skins for a bunch of humans."

I let the disgust drip from my voice, thick and oily as the memory of Caila's despair. "Caila is *nothing* like Uriel. She cares about the people here."

I REMEMBER her tears seven years ago.

"He's killing them. Everything I do to try and hide them, every bit of help I send... it's never enough. Nothing we do is ever enough."

October in Boston was dull grey skies and streets punctuated with slashes of red and orange and gold, like fire and blood. Caila paced through the cramped apartment like a caged animal while she waited for a phone call.

"Marianne, you can't keep hiding this from her. It's going to get both of you killed." Caila sat on the floor in the bare apartment, and the fact that she wasn't muttering about our lack of actual furniture showed me just how worried she was. Nothing existed beyond the voice on the other end of the phone. "I can't come. I know I'm being watched, and I'll lead him right to you. But you have to prepare her."

A day later, and it was over. It wasn't the first time either of us have had the bitter taste of failure burning in our mouths, but it was the first time I'd seen the perpetual optimism that Caila wore like a shield fall away.

GRACE TAKES A STEP FORWARD, sidestepping around Lucifer, and wraps her smaller hands around my own. I feel that same angelic lightness that floated around Caila, though Grace is tempered with a vein of darkness, black and strong as iron, and I stop being surprised that she managed to bring the Devil to his knees for love of her.

She's had an angel watching her from a distance since her birth. It only seems fitting that the Devil join the club.

"Someone took her." The words tumble out of me, and I feel like one of the women who show up on our doorstep, broken and lost and eager to spill out my life's story to the pretty blonde angel in front of me.

But Heavenly blood or not, Grace is no angel, and Lucifer

might be a changed man, but trust has never come easily to either of us. I don't expect that to change now.

His hand covers Grace's where she's clutching mine, and from the outside it looks like a comforting gesture, but I've known Lucifer far too long to expect that. His fingers brush the back of my hand, and I feel him searching through my mind, subtle as a snake, flipping through thoughts and hidden desires with ease.

At least at first.

I'm not the girl staring over the cliffs, watching the sails fade into white specks on the waves anymore, and two thousand years has siphoned away any mortal fears and replaced them with bluntness and nerve. Lucifer presses against my mental walls, searching for the chinks in my armor, and I push back just as forcefully.

A warning flashes in Lucifer's eyes before he takes a step back, breaking the contact between us, and I wonder just how many people outside of this room can taunt the Devil and walk away unscathed.

"Did you see enough to satisfy you?" I turn away from them both and the soothing cloud of Grace's presence drops away, bringing back reality like a shock of icy water.

Grace's grey eyes dart between the two of us, but she stays silent.

Lucifer gives me a tight nod, and as quickly as it appeared his suspicion dissipates. "I didn't expect you to have taken up with another angel after my wayward brother."

Nothing but a tick in my jaw betrays me as I clench my teeth to avoid reacting to the name Lucifer's dancing around. He, no doubt, saw the massive wall around my heart with Michael carved into every brick.

"That has nothing to do with this," I snap.

Lucifer sighs, turning his back on me and walking towards the kitchen, the soles of his shoes crunching on the chunks of glass still littering the floor. He crouches down and runs his fingertips over the scorch marks blackening the floor.

"That's where you're wrong."

Caila's feather rests on the kitchen counter, the pristine golden plume looking out of place among the domestic rubble. Lucifer picks it up, turning it over in his hand, his eyes slipping closed. I wonder, not for the first time, what history he shares with my best friend. Our differing allegiances always remained carefully unspoken between Caila and I.

"Hell doesn't have her."

My shoulders slump as that chance shatters. I'd hoped for a demon gone rouge. A fallen angel that resented Caila skirting a bit too close to the dark side. Even Lucifer himself taking vengeance on Uriel's garrison.

"If she's not in Hell, and she's warded from me on Earth that just leaves-"

"Heaven." We both turn to Grace when she speaks up. Immediately her eyes widen and she puts up two hands, stopping us both before we can speak. "Don't look at me. I'm pretty sure I'm not at the top of anyone's list for information in Heaven. And your friend aside, if I can go for the rest of my life without encountering anymore of those feathered dicks, I'll be a happy girl."

This time it's Lucifer's turn to snort with laughter, but his amusement fades quickly when he turns back to me. "She's right, you know. If she was working to undermine Uriel, one of his supporters might have taken it on themselves to punish her. Seems like everyone is taking over Father's duties as of late."

"Then it's over." The idea of never seeing Caila again, of losing another person to Heaven's politics and back-biting snuffs out that flame of rage smoldering in me.

Gone. Not because of me, but that barely matters anymore.

"Maybe not."

That hollow place inside me blazes to life at Lucifer's words, even though I know it's just false hope. "I'm powerful, but my spells can't breach Heaven."

Lucifer's lips twist into a smile, and I almost expect to see an apple in his hand. "No one needs to breach anything when you have someone who can come and go as they please. Now just who do you know in Heaven?"

He can't possibly be suggesting-

"Michael."

"No," I snap.

Lucifer arches one dark eyebrow. "I'm well aware of your feelings toward my brother, but you know as well as I do that if she's hidden in Heaven he is the only shot you have."

"No," I repeat. "Don't ask me again. I'll find another way." I push past the both of them, barely hearing the murmur of concern from Grace as I shove open the back door.

The backyard is a mess neither of us have put much of an effort into improving yet. The grass is a few inches too high to be respectable, the spindly pale green blades wrapping around the chain link fence. I sit down on the cracked cement of the steps, the rough stone warm from the heat of another 90-degree day. The sun hangs low on the horizon, a streak of orange barely visible between the tightly packed houses.

The girl I was wouldn't have been able to comprehend a place like this. Two thousand years and six thousand miles separates the person I am now from her, but some days I can still feel that lost child ghosting my steps.

I hear the screen door behind me creak open before slamming shut with a dull slap. Grace hesitates for an instant before sitting down next to me.

I don't look at her when I start speaking. I stare out at the horizon and the thin sliver of the sunset I can see between buildings. "The world's not a great place for women, even now. But when I was born, it was so much worse." Grace shifts beside me, and I wonder at myself for dredging this up.

I know I can't refuse Michael's help, if he's even willing to give it. If another angel has Caila, we'll need all the aid we can get. Lucifer will do what he can, but I can't pretend that his immediate loyalty lies with anyone but Grace. He won't risk her or himself to save another angel, and I can't blame him for that.

Hearing Michael's name, even thinking it, dredges up memories I've buried for centuries under a sharp tongue and sharper blades.

"I was born in Phoenicia, over two thousand years ago. You stop keeping track after the first few centuries." I hear Grace's breath catch next to me, and I glance over at her, quirking a smile at the surprise on her face.

"I should be used to it by now," Grace says, shaking her head slightly, as though taking more than a few weeks to grow accustomed to people tossing the word centuries into conversation is unheard of. "Lucifer just never seemed to be anything but exactly what he is, but you feel different."

I turn away from Grace again, focusing back on the fading rays of orange cutting though the yard. "That's because I am. I'm human. At least part of me still is."

Phoenicia

43 AD

SIDON.

I was born during a summer storm. The waves clawed against the cliffs like monstrous fingers intent to rip our village into the sea. My father used to say it was proof that I had cursed his family, but we were damned long before I was conceived.

I am not one of the lucky ones, born in the villas at the top of the hill, overlooking the small, squat dwellings in silent judgment. I am not one of those girls born into a gilded cage, a pampered life of soft hands and docile servitude. They live in a prison, just as I do, but I would gladly trade all my lofty dreams of freedom for a soft bed and a kind word.

We are poor, but that doesn't always equal misery. Even for my own sisters our lot in life isn't entirely dismal.

Just for me.

I have the misfortune of being the seventh daughter of a man with no sons. A dye-maker by trade, my father spends his days crushing the sea snails down to make the famous Tyrian purple dye that stains his hands the color of old wine to the wrists. The stink of rotting shellfish hangs around him, a decaying miasma that fits the ugliness of his soul.

And from the moment I take my first breath, he hates me.

It's my eyes.

I share the same dark hair as my parents and sisters, deep chestnut brown shot through with strands of bronze that catch the sun like faint streaks of fire. I will one day grow taller than all of them, even my father, but he has no way of knowing that when he holds my squalling infant body.

But my eyes.

Pale blue as the distant snow-capped mountains, the first time they open he curls his lips into a sneer and shoves me into the arms of one of my sisters. That is the first and last time he ever holds me.

If I'd been a boy, those eyes would have been a sign that I'd been blessed by the gods. I would grow to be a hero or a warrior, anything but another man spending his days shoulder deep in rotting shellfish. My father would spend his days peacocking with pride at his boy that bears the mark of the gods, gulping down the thick wine, satisfied with the knowledge that he'll be able to hitch his future to his infant son's.

But I'm not a boy. Since I lack that one all-important appendage between my legs, my existence is a curse. Another mouth to feed. Another bride-price to negotiate in a few years. Another voice added to the feminine din in his house.

And two pale eyes always watching.

I might have endured it if the hatred had only come from him. If I'd been wrapped in the warm love of my mother and sisters, I might have learned to suffer with a sweet smile, lapping up any scraps of affection dropped my way. Instead, my earliest memories of my mother are her glaring at me like my very existence is a betrayal. In her mind, I'm certain it is.

My father couldn't breed a boy, so my mother looked elsewhere for the seed that would bring her that all-important son. A clandestine affair with another man from our corner of the village would be too risky, but a bustling port like Sidon brings ships each day bearing endless streams of foreigners. Greeks and Romans fill the marketplace, greedy fingers snatching up the Tyrian purple cloth to clothe the wealthiest citizens, and even a few golden-haired barbarians from the north walk our streets.

I still imagine my mother, hiding her face in the folds of her cloak, her skin worn and lined far before her time from a hard life, mixing herself with the whores down at the docks hoping to catch the eye of a wandering sailor.

I doubt she even bothered learning the name of the man who would father her youngest child, and if I'd been male any differences would have been forgotten in the joy of finally *finally* having a son.

Instead, I'm just a reminder of a failed attempt at controlling her own future, and my father mutters constantly about how his house is cursed with faithless women.

It's no surprise I run whenever I have the chance.

From the time I can walk, I focus every bit of my childlike energy on escaping the too-close walls of our home. The rough-chiseled limestone never represented the comfort of hearth and home or the relative safety of quiet domesticity. To my younger self those walls are nothing but a prison.

The only good fortune I have is the complete apathy of my parents. No one notices or cares where I go, so each day I slip out of the house at sunrise and follow the worn paths upward. Each step takes me higher and higher as I duck through the market stalls, ignoring the voices of our neighbors shouting the virtues of their wares, eager to sell bread or cloth or fruit to the foreigners wandering the city.

Up and up I go, the rough gravel digging into my bare feet, the sand sliding through my toes. Dust clings to the ragged hem of the raw linen of my robes, but all I see is the horizon. When I reach the top, out of breath from running, I freeze, the unrelenting sun beating down on my head as I stare over the edge of the dizzyingly high cliff to the bright turquoise of the water below.

So far above the city, the stink of the dye vats and unwashed bodies fades to nothing. The constant drone of voices becomes nothing more than a faint hum in the distance, blocked out by the cries of seabirds riding the updrafts and the roar of the wind whipping through my ears.

I spend my childhood on those cliffs, watching the ships and longing for the freedom they represent.

I am twelve years old, and life has never been kind to me. I know my hope of boarding one of those ships and sailing to another world will never leave the realm of dreams and wishes. If I'd been a man, the army would take me across continents, the navy across the seas, but I'm only a girl destined to live and die within a few miles of where I was born.

I'm still too young to truly understand hate, but I hate that knowledge.

I know that my days of freedom are winding down. Soon I will be married off to whatever man my father can convince to take me, and I'll spend my days as a servant in my own house, flat on my back whenever he demands it, bearing his children until, my body worn out and used up, death will come for me.

I think by then I will welcome it.

But the gift that comes with living as a ghost in your own home is knowledge. No one ever bothers to shield me from the truth, so I hear it all.

A short, squat man with glittering black eyes and an oily smile sat at my father's table the previous night, counting out coins into a purse that he presses into my father's greedy hands. Feigning sleep on the thin pallet in the darkest corner of the room, I listen.

"You're making the right choice," the man says, his lip curling in disdain as he takes in his rough surroundings. A handkerchief flutters through his thick fingers, soaked in perfume, and he holds it under his nose as he tries to block out the ever-present stink of the dye that clings to the house. His beady eyes narrow as he stares into the dark corner where I presumably sleep. From the shadows, I stare back, pouring every drop of anger my young mind can muster into that glare.

I know who he is. Every city of our size has a flesh-peddler, and there is only one reason a man like him would lower himself to enter a house such as ours.

He is making a purchase.

He snatches the purse back, satisfied that my father has already gotten the taste of those jingling coins into his heart. "A girl that willful with those strange eyes. . ." his voice trails off as he squints into the darkness, no doubt expecting my eyes to glow like a beast's. "No one will marry her," he continues, tucking the coins away in the folds of his robe. "But my customers will only see the pretty face, and I'll have that willfulness whipped out of her if she doesn't obey."

My father nods, sticky wine sloshing over the side of the clay bowl he drinks from, his mind already counting the coins. The brothel-keeper rises from the creaking chair, and the both of them stumble outside, murmuring plans of bringing me to the brothel in three days.

I'd like to say I was stunned. I wish I'd had it in me to be shocked that my own father had just sold me into a short, miserable life as a whore for a handful of coins, but it only seems like the next progression in my grim existence. But for the first time, I have one clear word echoing in my mind.

No.

I've seen those women down by the docks – their scarred faces, their dead eyes. They are the ones cast aside, unwanted daughters or barren wives, spinster sisters or girls who simply didn't know their place. A few would stare back at me, brashly daring me to insult them, but most keep their eyes on the ground until a potential customer strolls by.

My father's cruelty stole my childhood. It isn't going to steal the rest of my life. And I know just how to save myself from that fate. Or more specifically who.

Every village has that one women living alone in a dilapidated hut at the edge of town. The men sneer at her and call her a witch, harsh words hiding a very real mantle of fear. The respectable women of the city hide their faces behind veils when they knock on her door, begging for a charm to entice a lover to stay or heal an ailing child.

Ours was called Amma.

She was old when my mother was young, wrinkles carved into her nut-brown skin like canyons.

When I knock at her door a few hours later, there is no surprise on her face.

"I wondered when you'd come," she says without preamble, turning her back on me and walking into the shadows of the hut without pausing to see if I follow. "I've been waiting for you since the day your mother came to me with a swollen belly and demanded to know if she carried a boy." She laughs, a rough cackle splitting her thin lips, and flips open a large wooden trunk. She moves like someone half her age, her hands steady as they sift through the trunk's contents. This is no feeble old woman, whiling away the days as she waits for death.

The bronze bowl she pulls out is finer than anything I've seen before, the angular markings of the text around the border nothing more than pretty decorations to me then.

She places the vessel on the rough-hewn table, the shining metal looking out of place on the scarred wooden surface. I watch silently as she pours wine into the bowl, thick and dark as old blood. With a speed I don't expect from her age, she snatches my hand up, and a thin dagger that she concealed in the folds of her robes slices across my palm.

I hiss and try to yank my hand back, but her grip is strong, far stronger than it should be. She holds my bleeding hand over the bowl, her dark eyes watching as three drops land on the smooth surface of the wine.

She releases me and steps back, nodding at the bowl. "Ask," she orders. At my confusion, she adds. "I could feel the power in you before you were born. It's sleeping, and you're the only one who can awaken it. You must ask for it."

I am twelve years old. In this world, I would be a child, but I haven't been a child in a very long time. I've seen too much, felt the difference in me brewing discontent like a poison. My entire life, I have never asked for anything for myself.

I lean over the bowl and stare into the blackness. I see my own reflection, but underneath it something ripples, waiting. I can already feel it uncoiling in me.

"I want–" I stumble over the words, years of making myself as small as possible, of staring at the ground, of being invisible war with the desire to finally be in control of my own destiny.

I stand straighter, pulling myself to the full height I try so hard to conceal and stare into the depths of the bowl. The surface shivers.

I want control. Power. Freedom. I whisper the words in my mind as the mixture smolders.

I want to choose my own way. The surface bubbles, and I feel the heat rising up.

No one will ever own me again. Ignition. All at once the wine erupts into flame, thick smoke rising from the surface and surrounding me. It pours into my lungs, and instead of choking the breath from me the heat feels cleansing, scouring my soul of weakness and fear, leaving those places open for something better.

The fire burns itself out quickly, consuming the fuel and leaving the bowl empty and gleaming on the table.

I feel the wood under my fingertips, felt the splinters where they dig into my palm. I taste smoke and blood, and I know I'm done asking. There will be no more begging for scraps.

I turn my attention away from the empty bowl, turning to Amma and finally meeting her eyes. She's smiling.

"What's next?"

4
MICHAEL

She's here.

Elissa is here.

Grace and Lucifer are laughably easy to find. Neither one makes any effort to conceal their presence, and the power rolling off them in waves can be felt for miles. I'm no stranger to my brother's pride, and I never expected to find Lucifer masking himself from Heaven, but the girl surprises me.

The Last is still such a contradiction to me. She walks beside Lucifer, her slight form looking so small and breakable and human. Her eyes pause on other mortals as they pass, their souls laid bare before her, and I wonder if she can feel the blackness tingeing her own.

Then she looks at my brother and the light that surges in her soul blocks out the darkness, and I can feel my own sin choking me.

Envy always was the ugliest of sins.

Its weak cousin jealousy pales in the face of what I feel looking at them. Jealousy merely means wanting what someone else has, but envy is wanting them not to have it.

To me, Grace holds no more enticement than any other human. Beautiful, yes, but nothing more than that until I see Lucifer's attention slide to her. I see the way his hand rests at the small of her back and his eyes follow her steps, and the longing catches in my throat. I remember the cliffs and the sand and the washed out blue of the summer skies, that hue still so much darker than her eyes.

And I want.

The structure they enter is nothing special, another low shotgun house with a fresh coat of white paint hastily applied to the worn siding and a slightly wilted pot of scarlet geraniums sitting sentry by the front door. The scent of magic hangs thick as smog in the air, and my hand unconsciously moves to my blade. I grip the handle, the familiar weight doing nothing to calm the uneasiness that crawls across my skin like insects, and I wonder if Grace and Lucifer can feel the twisted sense of wrongness emanating from the house.

Whatever happened here, it isn't good.

I keep my distance as the sun dips lower and the first streaks of purple begin to color the sky. I circle the small house and the overgrown backyard, keeping concealed in the shadows between the two neighboring houses when the back door bangs open and she emerges.

My Elissa.

But, of course, she hasn't been *my* Elissa in centuries, and this hard-edged creature that pauses on the bare cement slab of the back porch to scan the scraggly grass of the backyard hardly resembles her.

The petticoats and lace of Paris and the soft linen of Sidon are long gone, replaced by black denim and faded cotton. She dresses for utility now, for battle, a stark contrast to the filmy sundresses Grace seems to live in. If the heavy leather boots or dark jeans are uncomfortable in the stifling heat she doesn't show it. Elissa drops down to the steps, resting her head in her hands and sighing loudly. She looks upset, and my irrational heart wants nothing more than to comfort her.

I quash that urge before it can grow. Whatever emotions my presence might bring out of her, comfort is very far down the list.

The door creaks again and Grace emerges, hesitating in the doorway for several moments before sitting down next to her, delicately tucking her bare legs under the hem of the sky blue dress she wears. I almost want to laugh at the irony. The Prince of Darkness has his heart stolen by this picture of innocence with her sundresses and golden hair, while God's most obedient son can't look away from a glowering witch in biker boots.

Elissa starts speaking without looking at Grace. She keeps her voice a low murmur, flat and emotionless as she recounts the story of her childhood and the ugly, unloved existence she endured before I met her.

I listen, feeling like a voyeur as the words spill from her, but I'm too enthralled with this unknown side of her to do the honorable thing and leave. I forget myself, my all-important duty, everything but her measured voice weaving the image of her past.

What does it say that for everything we shared, she never shared these secrets with me? What does it say that I'd never thought to ask why she cloistered herself at the apex of the city, building her own gilded cage and feathering the nest with power?

When I walked into her life, Elissa was well on her way to becoming the witch she is now, wrapping herself in a mantle of blood magic and immortality until nothing and no one could touch her. Her power on Earth had grown enough that even Heaven took notice and as the only angel in the vicinity, I was sent to investigate.

Grace puts her hand on Elissa's shoulder, and I see the first crack in the armor surrounding her as she leans into the touch, that tiny movement as she seeks comfort revealing just how much digging up her early life pains her.

So much loneliness. So much regret.

I try to reconcile the picture of that barefoot child, alone and unwanted, with the women I knew so many years ago.

Did I really know her at all?

Phoenicia

53 AD

The house sits on the cliff side, as close to the edge as the masons dared build, and I suspect that more than a little magical help is shoring up the limestone. I land on a wide balcony that stretches over the dizzying precipice, nothing more than a stone railing holding you back from a sheer drop into the ocean far below. The wind whips my feathers and stings my eyes as I hide my wings and walk through the wide double doors into the atrium.

This is no rough hut outside the safety of the town where spell-casting might go unnoticed. This is no stinking fisherman's hovel when the lost and forgotten claw for any power they might find. The owner of this house has no fear of displaying her considerable wealth, and the privilege of building her home so high above the muck of the city shows that she has far more influence in this place than I expected.

The roar of the wind fades as I walk through the door, cloaking my presence from the mortals inside. Even with the wind silenced, the house is far from quiet. Servants bustle through the house, women young and old tending the household tasks with quick efficiency.

A girl of barely more than ten brushes past me, a basket overflowing with ripe fruit in her hands. I follow her, watching as she slips into the kitchen, passing the basket into the hands of the cook, a small woman with the same smile who could only be her mother. She was beautiful once, but half her face is marred with a deep burn, and I hear the echoes of her pain when the torch was thrust into her face.

Now she laughs as she digs through the basket before pulling out a pomegranate. Singing to herself, she cuts into the fruit, the ruby seeds spilling out like drops of blood. "Sisa, come here!" she calls, popping a few of the sweet seeds into her mouth before passing the fruit to the child. "Bring the figs to Tanith for the mistress." The child nods solemnly before gabbing up the basket and barreling out of the room, her mother's voice ringing through the corridor like a bell.

These are not the well-trained daughters of the domestic class, women working the only trades allowed to them. As I pass unseen through the servants I see a few scarred faces and even more scarred souls that belie their current happiness. The lives of these women were not easy before they came to this house on the cliffs, and the gratefulness in their hearts isn't for love of a soft bed in the beautiful house and the promise of a kind mistress.

She saved them all, in one way or another, and every one of them would kill for her.

I follow the child to a frail, elderly woman with a missing eye. Her gnarled hands hold a simple bronze tray with a cup of the harsh wine favored in this city. The girl proudly brandishes the basket of figs, rifling through them to search for the choicest morsels before depositing three fat figs onto the tray, their golden skin bursting with juices. "Back to your mother, Sisa," the old woman says. "I'll tell the mistress they came from you."

The child beams, revealing a gap-toothed smile that the old woman mirrors before running back down the hall, her small feet slapping on the clay tiles. Chuckling, the old woman taps gently on the door.

"Come in!" a muffled voice answers, and she pushes open the heavy wooden door.

Sunlight streams in through the high windows, the air clean and sharp from this height. Bundles of herbs hang down from the rafters, swaying in the soft breeze that flows through the windows, releasing their scents to fill the room.

A mountain of tightly rolled scrolls rests on the large wooden table in the center of the room. Maps are spread out on the surface, their edges curling, and other fragments of yellowed parchment, scribbled with text in Greek and Latin and Phoenician litter the surface.

I creep in behind the old woman, keeping my presence carefully cloaked, and take in the woman bent over the maps. The old woman walks closer, delicately placing the tray on a clear space beside her.

"Thank you, Tanith," she says, without looking up.

"Little Sisa picked the very best figs for you," she croaks, her voice a low rattle in her throat. Tanith pauses for a moment, as though considering her next words. "It's a lovely day outside, mistress. You've been shut up in this room for days." She rests one of her worn, wrinkled hands on the woman's arm and squeezes gently, the sort of casual touch one would see between a grandmother and a wayward child and not servant and mistress.

The younger woman looks up, her ice blue eyes focusing on the old woman for just a moment before flicking to where I stand by the doorway. "What have I told you about calling me mistress?" she asks, her full lips curling into a smile that I know she means for me. "It's Elissa." Her voice is firm, but kind, repeating a conversation that has likely occurred many times before. "Fortune has been kind to me in these last years, but I am no one's master."

She looks away from me and focuses on Tanith, and the old woman smiles at her, revealing a mouth with far more gaps than teeth. "I promise, I'll come out soon. And do tell Sisa I thank her for the figs. She always knows which are the sweetest." Her eyes slide back to my hiding spot, locking with my gaze, and she adds, "For now though, I've just found something very interesting that I need to look into."

Neither of us look away from the other as Tanith totters out of the room, closing the heavy door behind us with an audible click.

Elissa is on her feet an instant later, striding across the room towards me. She holds my gaze, her steps sure and steady and without fear, and I indulge myself for a moment.

She is tall, her back ramrod straight when she stands. As with everything else in the house, her attire speaks of wealth without ostentation. The robes she wears are soft linen of the purest white. The fabric she drapes herself in is undoubtedly fine and many steps removed from the rougher spun cloth the servants clothe themselves in, but any man or pampered wife in the city holding court in a household such as this would have been decorated in the famous Tyrian dye, yet I haven't noticed a stitch of purple anywhere in the house.

The nimble fingers of her servants have twisted her dark hair into a nest of elaborate braids that coil like snakes around her skull before dangling down her back. Anyone else would have dripped with jewels and gold, but only a few simple bracelets of hammered bronze circle her slim wrists. Beyond that, she is unadorned. She needs nothing else.

She stands before me, her icy blue eyes staring up into mine, and she presses her hand against my chest, pushing just hard enough to rock me back on my heels in surprise. "And who are you?"

Magic crackles around her, leaving the air charged as in the moments before a lightning strike, and if I have any reservations left that she is the one I seek they melt away.

Her finger pokes impatiently into my chest again, reminding me that her question still hangs unanswered.

"I am the Archangel Michael."

Elissa takes a step backward, cocking her head to the side as she takes my measure. She narrows her pale blue eyes for a moment as she mulls over my words. "A servant of the new god then," she says, turning her back on me and returning to her maps and parchments. I gape at her as she grabs a fig from the tray and takes a delicate bite, the sticky sweet juice running over her lips as she glances back at me, unconcerned.

"Now tell me, Archangel Michael," she demands, the casual disinterest fading abruptly as she drops the half-eaten fig onto the clay plate. "What is your business in my home?"

I don't have an answer. My orders were to merely observe this woman, to watch and discover the depths and heights of her abilities. What has she bartered with to claim this power? Has she been trading with the Fallen or with Lucifer himself?

It's obvious that she is no village healer dealing only in herbs and trinkets. These are old magics swirling around her, power born from blood and fire and the Earth itself.

But I feel no evil in her. No true darkness. Her affection for the old woman has lit up her soul, and even now I see no anger or fear in her, nothing but a curiosity and a mild annoyance at my unexpected interruption.

"Have you forgotten how to speak?" she asks, a chuckle in her voice. "Whatever the men in the village might say, I don't wrest the tongues from men to boil into my potions." A spark of resentment flickers across her soul at that, a contradiction to the lightness of her tone.

I evidently am not the first man to show up at Elissa's door questioning her, but I suspect I'm the first to make it past her threshold.

"I have no quarrel with you, witch," I say, finally leaving my spot on the periphery of the room where I hung back silently observing.

"That's certainly a relief," Elissa replies, taking a sip of her wine as she unrolls another scroll, the parchment covered in cramped Greek letters.

I've never come across a mortal like her. Witch or not, I'm an Archangel, and I could crush her out of existence with no more effort than swatting an insect, and yet here she sits, sipping wine and reading through her scrolls as though I'm nothing more than a passing merchant, boring her with my very presence.

"You have been noticed in Heaven."

Her muscles tense, the casual posture she slipped into tightening, and the flush of anger that pulses in her soul startles me.

"I've been noticed in Heaven," she parrots, slowly setting the cup and scroll back down onto the table, her movements suddenly stiff. "Of course, Heaven notices me now when all the gods were blind to my prayers when I was weak."

She rises from her seat and stalks across the room to the window, pushing open the half closed shutters that dampen the wind. Behind her, the scrolls flutter on the table like wings.

"You saw Tanith." Her back is to me as she stares out the window, her eyes focused on the distant horizon. "She was lucky enough to bear sons, but they left to seek their fortunes across the sea and forgot her. And when her husband died, she had nothing. I found her begging in the streets, living on whatever scraps she could find. Where was Heaven then?"

I keep silent. The wind whips through the room as I

creep closer to her. The scrolls flap upwards, her carefully arranged piles of parchment riding the drafts for a moment before faltering and dropping to the floor.

She stares unflinchingly into the stinging wind as she continues. "I'm sure you saw Sisa and her mother as you skulked through my house." Her hand grasps the windowsill, wood and stone creaking ever so slightly under her fingers as she fights for control. "Melita worked in the brothel," she murmurs, her voice nearly swallowed up by the wind. "Sisa was born there and would have continued in her mother's footsteps if I hadn't brought them here, but one of Melita's lovers was a jealous man. She was so beautiful, you see."

Elissa's voice trails off for a moment before she turns to face me, her anger barely held in check as she rails at me. "He didn't like sharing her, and he made her many pretty promises. But Melita refused to leave her daughter behind, and he didn't like that. If she wouldn't give herself solely to him, he made certain that no one else would want her. Where was Heaven then?"

The word blasphemy rests on my lips, and I wonder what outcome my Father expected from sending me here to be scoured by her righteous rage. Why had her little kingdom on the cliffside reached His notice?

Elissa shakes her head in disgust at my silence. The wind at her back tears at her hair, tugging dark strands free from her braids to swirl around her face as she stares coldly at me.

"Heaven was always there."

Something in her face softens at that, her lush lips curling into a sad smile. "And that, Archangel Michael, is exactly why I have no need of it."

A HAND CLAMPS down on my shoulder, wrenching me deeper

into the shadows between the two houses. I have my weapon in my hand in an instant, pressing against the neck of my assailant, ready to strike as I turn-

-and see the smug face of my brother looking utterly unconcerned with my blade digging into his throat.

"Michael," he drawls, his eyes flickering down to the blade. "At ease, solider." I lower the weapon reluctantly, stowing it away and glancing back to where Grace and Elissa still sit, unaware of both of us.

Lucifer follows my gaze, and I can feel his hackles rising as he connects the dots. "Why are you here?" he grinds out. "Did Father send you? Are you bringing another war to my doorstep?"

"Your doorstep?" I snap. "This isn't your world, Lucifer. We aren't meant to walk in this realm for long!" I sound entirely unconvincing, especially as I hide in the shadows like a love-struck human, mooning over a woman who loathes me.

Lucifer's anger melts into another self-satisfied grin, and I wrestle with the ever-increasing urge to punch him.

He was so much easier to deal with when he was just my mortal enemy.

"You'd know about over-staying your welcome, wouldn't you?" At my continued silence, Lucifer adds, "Do you honestly think things will go well for you if she sees you?"

The gravel crunches behind me, and I know without looking that it's her. Nothing more than the faintest intake of breath gives her away, a sharp inhale revealing her shock at seeing me. Two millennia have given her the iron control her younger self never had, and when I turn around to look her in the face for the first time in so long it's like staring into the dead eyes of a statue.

A slight tick as her jaw tightens is the only indication that my presence has any kind of effect on her. Beyond that, her face stays a mask as she pushes past me in the narrow pathway. Lucifer steps aside, and she pauses just long enough to give him a withering look before her boots are thumping on the uneven pavement of the sidewalk. A moment later I hear the low rumble of a motorcycle engine as she peels out, leaving me in a cloud of exhaust and confusion.

5
ELISSA

I ride without purpose.

The wind whips down my back, knotting my hair into a mass of snarls I'll be untangling for hours, but I can't bring myself to care. My helmet's somewhere back in the house, abandoned in the entryway, kicked aside and forgotten when I saw the rubble of the living room.

Usually I'm not this careless. Immortality for me isn't quite the same beast as for the angels. I don't age, and I'm immune to human sickness, but I can still be killed.

The odometer creeps upward as I tear through the wards, weaving in and out of traffic, ignoring the honking horns and yells of mortals trying to beat me at the road rage game.

Not tonight.

Two thousand years.

Two thousand years since the last time I saw him.

I shut down my mind, shoving those memories back into the impenetrable box they threaten to escape from. Opening up locked boxes didn't go so well for Pandora, and while evil already coats the world without my assistance I don't feel like revisiting that particular history lesson.

Instead I roll on the throttle a bit more and try to forget everything but the engine purring.

The city flies by in a blur of streetlamps and headlights. It's full dark now, and I've long since left the tourist areas. The streets of the Lower 9th Ward are mostly barren of other cars. I narrowly miss a pothole deep enough for its own zip code, and I feel my front tire wobble just a bit as the pebbles and broken pavement catch under my wheel.

I don't know if a crash at 90 miles an hour would be enough to end me, but I'm not eager to test the theory tonight.

I slow down, the roar of the engine fading to a murmur as I slide to a stop in the middle of the overgrown street.

The floodwall looms in front of me, thirty feet of concrete and steel waiting as a silent sentry to hold back the next hurricane. A billion dollars worth of human persistence rose this marvel on the back of the failed levee while the bones of the Lower 9th Ward still rot around us.

I always seem to end up here.

I cut the engine of my bike, the sudden quiet jarring. The water of the canals laps against the floodwalls, bringing with it the muddy brine of the Mississippi, the smells of decaying vegetation washed in from the bayous overpowering the hint of jasmine riding the breeze.

I always run to places like this, the harbors and waterfronts, the dirty forgotten piers that stink of dead fish and moldering dreams. The witch Elissa was birthed on the cliffs, high above the stench of the dye huts and the choking poverty that came with them, but the human girl Elissa?

She was born here.

The houses in New Orleans might not look the same as what I was raised in, but I see a thousand faces that could have been my family, barely eking out a living on crumbs.

And when all you have are crumbs, someone's bound to go hungry.

Michael.

I choke down the sob that threatens to escape my throat.

Why is he here? Why now?

I heard all the rumors. He was in the thick of it down here, actually working side by side with Lucifer to stop Uriel, but once the dust settled he was back knocking on the Pearly Gates, leaving the rest of us to clean up after Heaven's mistakes again.

Or so I thought.

I want the years to show on his face. I want the time that has passed to have left some kind of mark, some scar on his soul glowing like a beacon and reminding me that what we had wasn't just something I dreamed up during a balmy summer night.

I loved him once. Loved him so much that for the first time in my life I'd been able to bury my past and ignore my future. I wasn't the witch or the mistress.

I was Elissa. Just Elissa.

But I wasn't enough.

And now Michael is here.

God's battering ram is still wrapped up in the same appealing package, as though his almighty Father was just setting out a lure to lead the weak humans into ruin.

The robes are gone, traded in for worn jeans and a grey t-shirt. The hair that hung in the soft blond waves I spent nights tangling my fingers through is shorn close to his head, making his blue eyes even brighter, the deep indigo of the sea at dusk. Two thousand years, and I see his arms, see those thick muscles that could tear down city walls, and all I remember is the sensation of them coiled around me, holding me close enough that his scent still surrounds me, that clean ozone smell that always says *angel*.

I've always been immensely thankful that Caila's infatuation with everything we humans create extends to expensive floral perfumes. The heady scents of jasmine and magnolia that waft around her make her appear even more like a debutante slumming it with a bad influence like me, but they're just enough to hide that essence of Heaven that clings to every angel.

But Caila isn't here to listen to my burdens and offer the best friend duty of hating my ex with a vitriol exceeding even mine, and for all that I'd been willing to share the dirty details of my mortal life with Grace, I can't share this with the woman that Lucifer chose and fought for.

Not when I was the one left behind.

My foot brushes a broken chunk of pavement, and I crouch down and grab it. The jagged piece of asphalt and cement digs into my fingers, leaving dirty streaks across my palm, and I lob it against the floodwall with all my strength. It disintegrates into dust and pebbles on impact, and I drop to my knees next to my bike, the momentary pleasure of destruction fading as the realization that I have to go back sets in.

Caila's still missing, trapped by someone with enough power to bind an angel and blind my spells. My feelings, my memories, twenty centuries of hating him. . . none of it matters as much as freeing her. Michael owes me this, and if I have to dredge up that buried pain for his help, I will.

Caila's out there, and I might not be able to find her on my own, but a witch, the Devil, the Last, and an Archangel searching for her? Whoever took my friend doesn't stand a chance.

THE HOUSE IS dark when I pull up, and I'm not surprised. I

don't doubt that Michael is lurking nearby, mentally scourging himself while he tries to figure out what to say to me, but he keeps himself well hidden.

I can't blame him for wanting to delay the inevitable confrontation. After two thousand years, "How've you been?" falls pretty flat.

I push open the unlocked door and flick on a light. The rubble of our house is unchanged, and I wrinkle my nose in annoyance as I grab a broom and start sweeping up the worst of the damage, all the while scanning the house for any microscopic clue I might have missed.

Nothing. Broken glass and scorched furniture aside, whoever was here covered their tracks well.

For the sake of thoroughness, I enter Caila's room. At every location, Caila feathers her nest immediately, trying on different aesthetics and discarding them just as easily. *Things* appeal to her so much that it makes me wonder what sort of drab, beige existence she must have lead in Heaven that causes her to be so utterly fascinated by the world of home décor.

A low platform bed made of artfully aged wood takes up half the room, the mattress covered by a fluffy comforter she dragged home a few weeks ago, all the while crowing over her love of "millennials and their pink." A console table of sleek gold and glass looks out of place holding up a stack of thick leatherbound books older than this house. The small closet is no match for Caila's attire so a large wardrobe hugs the back wall, the ornately decorated wood whitewashed into a pale cream.

At first glance the room is untouched, and I nearly flip off the light and leave, but something makes me pause and stare at the wardrobe a bit closer.

Something is off.

I squint, stepping into the room, and then it dawns on

me. The wardrobe juts out from the wall an inch or so, making it look off-kilter in the flawless order of the room.

I curl my fingers in between the thick plywood backing and the wall and pull, gritting my teeth at the grating noise as it rubs along the floor.

Hidden behind the wardrobe is a circle painted in blood, the jagged zigzags in the center completing the sigil. I take a step closer, holding my hand over the surface and feel the same echo of power that choked me when I scryed for Caila.

I know this mark. I've used it more than once myself. Written in blood, it dampens the powers of any angel in its proximity. Caila would have still been stronger than a human, but the sudden weakness would have left her confused and off-balance, giving her attacker a serious advantage.

It also tells me something else, something far more important.

No angel, fallen or not, could use this sigil without weakening themselves as well.

Her attacker is human.

BLOOD LEAVES A TRAIL.

Most magic isn't picky. Blood is blood, and squeezing it from a willing or unwilling donor is the mystical equivalent of filing the serial number off a gun. If you bother doing it, there's probably a reason you don't want to be found.

But some spells are different. Magic isn't just some passive force that can be harnessed and controlled like electricity. Knowing all the rules and pretty incantations might be enough to heal or kill or even amass a tidy fortune, but real power. . . ancient power demands a tribute. It demands blood and bone and just a bit of your soul.

I press my hand against the sigil, the drying blood still

tacky under my palm, even hours later, and I fight back the urge to recoil at the blackness that washes over me when I make contact.

I'm no angel. I can't read sins and souls with a glance or a touch. For all my abilities, the secret thoughts and hidden desires of those around me stay shuttered, but that doesn't mean I'm blind.

It's like being doused in oil, thick and black, and my lungs close up as some animal part of my brain tries to shield itself from breathing this darkness in. The deep burgundy soaking into the wall looks deceptively normal. . . deceptively human. And while this person might be human on paper anything resembling actual humanity is a ship that sailed long ago.

My burning lungs give up, and I breathe in and almost retch at the putrid smell that fills my nose. I grew up by the ocean long before the advent of indoor plumbing. I'm no stranger to odors that would make most modern humans shudder, but this. . . this is the cloying scent that hung in the air during the plague, the sickly sweet miasma of decomposition, a soul-deep putrescence that has seeped into her very blood.

Her.

I blink, trying ineffectually to clear the haze from my eyes, pushing back into the visions swirling around me even as every part of me cringes back. But I have to be sure.

There are many ways to immortality and none of them are pretty or easy. All of them leave scars, but that's to be expected. If living forever was easy, no one would ever die.

I made choices and sacrifices for my long life that others might balk at, but nothing like this.

The owner of the blood has carved off chunks of herself in trade for her long life, feeding bits of her soul to whatever creatures wanted a taste until what's left behind is black as tar. She's human only on the barest of technicalities, and she has Caila.

My vision swims, and I try to claw my way past the pitch thick curtain veiling my eyes. Every sane part of me rebels against the evil touching me, but deep deep underneath it all, I hear a whisper sweet as poisoned honey beckoning me closer.

"You wanted this. You wished for this. You dreamed of watching Heaven burn. What is one more dead angel?"

My knees buckle and my hand slips off the wall, breaking contact just enough to throw me out of the vision. When my eyesight clears, I'm on my hands and knees next to Caila's wardrobe, coughing and retching, trying not to throw up at what I saw, what I felt. My skin crawls. I feel filthy, like I touched something so vile, so deeply tainted that nothing can scour me clean again. I squint at my hands, trembling as they barely hold me up, and I'm almost surprised that they're not coated in blacked blood.

Shakily, I get to my feet, grabbing the edge of the wardrobe to steady myself. I feel drunk, and not in a pleasant way. Everything spins in and out of focus, and the sickness in the pit of my stomach shows no signs of fading. I feel wrong, and I want to crawl into the shower and scrub myself down to my bones, even though I know nothing but time will ease this.

Caila's bed beckons like a soft cloud of dusty pink and white, and it takes every ounce of resolve I can muster to put one foot in front of the other and stagger out the door. Every step gets a bit easier, and by the time I reach the front door, I can at least feign normalcy.

I don't have much time. The tenuous link between Caila's abductor and myself is already starting to unravel, thread after thread snapping as my body purges itself from her twisted magic. If I'm going to find her, I need to follow the bond before it breaks entirely because I can't go back in there.

If we stay in this house, I'll rip out that wall before I touch that blood again.

I climb onto my bike, and I bite back a laugh as I send out a silent prayer to whatever might be listening that I don't crash before I find Caila.

If seeing Michael drove me to reckless riding earlier, what I just witnessed increases that tenfold. Heedless, I barrel through the streets, cutting in and out of traffic, blowing through red lights, and narrowly missing a stretch Hummer double-parked outside a club.

My focus is pinpoint tight, following the tug of magic, and I know I'm more than likely sprinting headlong into a trap. None of that matters though. Nothing matters but finding Caila.

I slam on the rear brake, gripping the handlebars tightly as my rear wheel fishtails out before sliding to a stop. I blink, true awareness coming back to me for the first time since I touched that wall.

The last tenuous link that drew me here snaps, and I let go of a breath I didn't realize I'd been holding. The sick feeling in the pit of my stomach hasn't entirely disappeared, but with every exhale the sensation of being unclean fades a bit more.

Looming in front of me is no dilapidated Victorian, no Stephen King dream that might as well advertise "creepy things inside" with a neon sign. And we're a long way from my side of town where the long, low houses give way to decaying warehouses and abandoned storefronts.

Instead a stately mansion rises up from behind a ten-foot high iron fence. Thick columns support the porch, connected by an ornate iron railing, the whorls and twists of the metal tangled with jasmine creeping up the side of the house. Two large crepe myrtle trees flank the pathway to the front door, the branches so heavy with deep pink flowers that the tree looks like it's burning in the dim light.

It looks like every other impeccably manicured mansion on this street. To anyone else it would look like another bed and breakfast catering to the tourists that have outgrown Bourbon Street or a monument to old money and antebellum decadence.

The heady scent of jasmine is thick in the air, and it reminds me of the delicate bouquets the wealthy waved beneath their noses during the black plague. But a perfumed corpse is still a corpse and this house with its pampered flowerbeds and neatly trimmed lawn stinks of corruption to anyone with perception.

Layer upon layer of wards and spells surround the house. Spells to hide its location from angels and demons alike, spells to weaken any unlucky enough to cross the threshold, spells to sound an alert when an unwelcome visitor treads on the doorstep – they wind and tangle together, part of one sigil forming another and another, encircling every square inch inside the fence with an impenetrable snarl of dark magic.

This is bad.

This is so fucking bad.

"Elissa."

I tense. It shows just how off balance I am that I didn't even register Michael's presence until he spoke. I know I need all the backup I can muster to even consider breaking Caila out of this mystical prison, but I feel the remnants of the toxic magic still flowing through my veins, loosening the tightly reined anger I spend so much effort containing.

I turn on Michael, and at the first sight of him my traitorous, weak heart threatens to soften. Two thousand years and everything about him is different, but he's still so beautiful, and I nearly falter as it all rushes back to me. The centuries of missing my hands in the blond locks of hair, the soft linen of his robes against my bare skin, the taste of honeyed wine on his lush lips.

The strong line of his back as he walked away.

"He left you. You weren't enough. You were never enough."

I want to blame that whisper on the spell, on some scrap of dark magic still clinging to my soul, but I know those words are nothing but my own insecurities and regrets.

It always was so much easier to be angry than hurt.

"Why are you here?" My voice is even. Cold. I lift my chin, staring upward at those sad eyes. Michael flinches ever so slightly at my tone, and I almost smile at his discomfort.

Good.

"I was sent here."

I exhale, the noise somewhere between a laugh and a snort. "I don't know why I expected anything else," I mutter. Another mission. Of course. What else would bring him back?

He opens his mouth to speak, but I cut him off with a raised hand. His mouth snaps closed so quickly it's almost comical.

God's most fearless warrior indeed.

Being this close to Michael throws me back to so many years ago, and I want to wipe that sad puppy look off his face. I want to hate him, and the look of contrition he wears like a shroud makes it difficult.

"Centuries," I spit, "It's been centuries, Michael, and you end up here. Now." I brush against the fence and anger spikes through me like a shot of adrenaline, blotting out everything but the red haze that crests in my soul as I stare at Michael. "I have more important things than you to concern myself with right now."

"Elissa, just let me explain. Please." Michael's hand brushes my arm, and the contact jolts us both. Michael's hands close around my shoulders and he yanks me away from the fence. The contact breaking is like a bucket of icy water splashing over my head, immediately quelling the rage that smolders like the beginnings of a wildfire.

Michael staggers, leaning heavily against me. "The fence," he murmurs. He cranes his neck to look over my shoulder, and his eyes widen as he sees the spells and wards covering the grounds. He takes a step backward, keeping a good foot between us and the fence.

I don't know how I missed it before. What wraps around the fence isn't a spell. It's a trapped soul, blackened and evil, bottled inside warded iron until just a touch is enough to corrupt.

Michael sways on his feet, and I know the dark magic surrounding us is sapping his strength.

I almost don't hear it. If it had been daytime and the endless klaxon of traffic and voices was flowing around us in a tide of unceasing human noise, I would have missed it. But tonight the streets are silent and the quiet ping as a crossbow fires reaches my ears, and I react with milliseconds to spare, shoving Michael to the left.

I'm still not fast enough. The bolt barely misses his heart, burying itself deep into his chest, and Michael drops like a stone.

If he'd been human, tearing the bolt from his body would do nothing but make him bleed out faster, but I don't have to touch the bolt to know it was forged in Hell. Every second it touches him, it does more damage.

I grip the end of the bolt, the black metal slippery with blood, and yank it out. Michael moans, a low, animal sound of pain that I can't reconcile with the warrior I knew.

I glance over at the house, expecting another projectile to fly out any moment. Buried somewhere in the briar patch of magic is the same ward on the wall of my house. Maybe more than one. I need distance for Michael to heal.

I hook my arm under Michael's shoulder and drag him to his feet. He's barely more than dead weight, and I certainly can't balance him on the gas tank of my motorcycle like a prized buck.

I drag him across the street, all the while bracing myself for an attack that doesn't come, the walk of a few short feet taking an agonizingly long time as every cracking branch when the breeze shifts becomes another assault.

Across the street is another mansion, the windows black and silent as the residents rest in the easy sleep of the unaware. I wonder if sharing a street with a murderous witch has any effect on property values.

Luck is on my side for once. A sedate grey sedan sits in front of the house, the automotive equivalent of elevator music, but right now it's a chariot from the gods because the door to the backseat is unlocked.

Thank goodness for careless rich people.

I maneuver two hundred and fifty pounds of barely conscious angel into the backseat, thankful I don't have to waste time and risk drawing more attention to myself by breaking a window. Michael slumps down, leaving a red smear on the cream leather.

The wound isn't healing. Even with a Hell forged blade, the wound should already be starting to knit itself back together. I wrap my hand around his face, cupping his jaw, and forcing his head up. "Michael. Michael, look at me," I demand, trying to keep my voice steady. He peels his eyes open slowly, squinting as he tries to focus on me.

"Elissa? What?" His brow furrows, and the confusion in his blue eyes is terrifying. Archangels are resolute, as powerful as the seasons, as unyielding as the tides. They don't stare up at you and ask in a small, slurred voice, "Are we at home?"

I let go of him, easing him back against the seat, and buckle the seatbelt across his chest, telling myself that it's just adrenaline making my hands shake.

I straighten up and slam the back door before climbing in the front seat, ripping open the front panel and digging through the wires for the two I need. A moment later, the engine is rumbling as I peel down the street.

Home. Even delirious and half-conscious, I know he's thinking of the villa, and I let the memory of waves crashing against the cliffs and seabirds shrieking in the wind drown out the pained gasps coming from the backseat each time the tires jolt over uneven pavement.

The only place that was ever truly mine, and Michael is calling it home.

It's just the pain talking.

He doesn't know what he's saying.

It's been too long, and there's far too much history between us.

I glance back in the mirror and watch him breathe, and I push the gas pedal harder.

6

MICHAEL

"What the Hell did you do to him?"
"Don't play the dutiful brother now, Lucifer. You know this wasn't me."
"Then *what happened?*"

I'm drifting. Their voices slide over me like waves, and I fight against the current trying to draw me away from them. Elissa. Lucifer.

My love. My brother. Bonded together in their mutual hatred for me.

I open my eyes for a moment and see Lucifer standing over me, head bent as he examines the bloody crossbow bolt in his hand. He glances up for the barest instant and almost drops the bolt in surprise at seeing my eyes open. "Michael!" he exclaims, his hand reaching toward me. "Brother, can you hear me?"

My eyes drift shut as I'm pulled back under.

Phoenicia
53 AD

I DON'T UNDERSTAND why I return to this place a second time. The witch isn't evil. Her scrolls and maps hide no plans to wrest power from Heaven or corrupt innocent souls. Her power burns bright enough that even Heaven sees its beacon, but she uses that light to heal and to protect those weaker than her.

She deserves peace and freedom from the celestial quarrels she wants no part in. I know I should leave her be and return to my post, but instead I find myself back in that bright room, watching as she continues to pour over scroll after scroll. She glances up when I enter the room, her lips quirking upward for just a moment before she composes herself.

"Back again?" she asks, her voice light.

I nod, not trusting myself to say anything of coherence when I don't understand myself why I returned.

"Then come in and stop hiding in doorways and shadows. Sit. I'll have Tanith bring wine."

"There's no need," I try to interrupt, but she waves one hand in dismissal, her long fingers cutting through the air.

"Nonsense," she continues. "I don't get many visitors, and certainly not many angels. Let me play the gracious lady of the house for a few hours." Her eyes sparkle at her own joke, and I think of what waits for me when I return to Heaven. More orders, more wars and executions. More blood on my hands.

Elissa rises from her seat, impatience at my hesitation plainly written across her face. She takes my hand and leads me back to the bench, and I'm so taken aback by her boldness that I follow, docile as a child.

"Sit," she repeats, dropping down on the cushioned seat

beside me. I still feel the heat of her fingers around my wrist like a brand. She cocks her head to the side as she watches me. "Are all of your kind so very strange or is just you?" she asks. Without waiting for a reply, she picks up one of her maps and begins regaling me with tales of the spice traders and merchants she has investments in.

The words tumble out of her, unhurried but showing no signs of stopping, and I wonder how long it has been since she was able to speak to someone she considers an equal. Her fondness for the women that fill the house is apparent, but they view her as some untouchable goddess saving them from lives of misery and deprivation.

Elissa speaks of the ships with such longing. "I want to go where they go," she murmurs, her fingers tracing over the broad lines of trade routes crisscrossing the map. "One day soon, I will see the world."

BLACKNESS. I surface through the memory, Elissa's voice fading into the frantic whispers of another woman. *Grace,* some part of my brain supplies. *Lucifer's Grace.*

"I don't know why it isn't working. I healed Phenex. I healed you. Elissa, I'm sorry. . ."

"It's not your fault." Lucifer's voice is firm, but far gentler than I ever expected from him. When he speaks again though, the voice I hear is not my brother, not Lucifer, but purely the Devil. "Where is she?"

PHOENICIA

53 AD

ELISSA KISSES ME FIRST, and it's a shock and completely expected at the same time. Each day I come, trailing her through the grounds and watching her with the rest of the household until she forbids me from dogging her heels until I make myself visible.

I comply without much argument, and the one-eyed old woman claps her hands together when she meets me, smiling with gap-toothed glee and cackling about the mistress' handsome suitor.

Elissa smiles that familiar secret smirk, but doesn't comment. When I don't immediately refute Tanith's words, I notice she stands a bit closer to me, and those brief touches begin to linger.

I am not naïve, nor am I am blind to the ways of humanity, but these feelings that surge in me when she is near are new.

In the hours when I am away from her, when I soar across the seas or to the highest peaks, gazing down from dizzying heights upon my Father's creation, I find my mind wandering back to Elissa. She would marvel at the vast expanse of the blue ocean, silent but for the wind buffering my wings a mile from shore. The sun blazes down on my back, and I know I could keep flying, my wings tearing through mile after mile until I reach another land.

I want to share all of it with her.

She asks nothing of me. When I have revealed my presence to mortals in the past, the clamor of fear or the incessant begging for blessings and healing overwhelmed me. But Elissa needs none of that. Instead, she asks only for companionship, and even that is not spoken aloud.

What grows between us is no more than the smallest seed at this point, easily trampled by carelessness or uprooted by the whims of nature, but with each day it grows stronger. The hours spent outside her presence grow fewer and fewer until one day, as the sun dips below the horizon, and I stand on the balcony, my wings already catching the updraft she blurts out, "You could stay."

And I do. I fold my wings and follow her through the door, shutting the wind and the skies and the rest of the world outside. Angels have no need for sleep, and I have never though of home as anyplace but Heaven. Yet now I watch the sway of her hips as she walks a few steps ahead of me down the corridor, and for the first time I understand those of my brothers and sisters who fell to temptation on this plane.

I hesitate. She walks a few more steps before she notices the absence of my footfalls behind her. She turns, the soft white of her robes flaring out behind her. *Like wings,* my mind supplies.

But no, Elissa has no wings, is no angel. She is of this earth. She is blood and bones and even with the magic coursing through her veins, she is still so human. I should feel nothing for her but the same aloof affection I feel for all my Father's creations.

I should not hear my own breath catch as she stands before me, so close I can smell the twin scents of smoke and incense that cling to her hair. She says nothing, only stares at me with those pale blue eyes. I can feel the want rise up in her, see the deep red flush of her soul, that hidden fire that I know will consume me. I feel as though I'm teetering at the edge of a precipice as I look at her. It's such a long way down, but I don't care.

She rises up on her toes and presses her lips against mine. I falter for the briefest moment, remembering Lucifer's burning wings as he fell and the blood on my hands as I slew my own siblings and the half-mad shrieks of the Nephilim.

I'm so tired.

Since even before the Fall, I've been God's Wrath, God's

Blade, God's Fists. After watching my return from battle after battle, my skin soaked in gore from dispatching the Fallen that were once our family, the other angels began giving me a wide berth.

Some small treacherous part of me misses those first days when Lucifer was still the Lightbringer, before Uriel retreated to his garden, and Raphael lost himself in his books and potions, and Gabriel fell silent.

This witch, this beguiling creature who shows no fear when she looks at me makes me feel like I belong. I didn't realize how much I missed that.

If this is how I fall, so be it.

I deepen the kiss, pulling her lithe frame against me, and a soft noise of surprise escapes her throat. She's like a deer, all long, slender limbs pressing against mine, ready to run if I give her any reason.

One of her hands creeps upward, those long, graceful fingers sliding through my hair to rest at the base of my skull, and I crush her closer. Her heart thrums against my chest, fast as a bird, as she pulls back just long enough to take a breath.

I follow her, chasing her lips with my own. She's happy to be caught, and the perpetual hum of noise in the villa fades to nothing as I lose myself in her.

The constant need for touch is something we all notice in Heaven. So many of us deride the foolish humans the way they endlessly rut against each other like beasts, obsessed with the base sensations of their weak flesh.

I wonder if my brothers and sisters are watching me now, gaping in shock as the mighty Michael is brought to his knees by a kiss.

"Michael." I open my eyes. I don't remember closing them. They slipped shut of their own volition as I lost myself in the tactile sensations of Elissa. My Elissa.

"Michael," she repeats, drawing my focus to her.

She has always been beautiful, but now with a flush across her cheeks and her lips red and bitten, she's stunning. We're both breathing hard, and somewhere in the last few moments she ended up with her back against the wall.

Her hand is still curled around my neck, those fingertips still stroking my skin, and I wonder for the barest moment if she is powerful enough to ensnare an angel.

It's nothing more than a foolish, idle thought, and I've forgotten it before it manages to take form. Her powers do not enchant me. I do not marvel over curses and spells any more than she is awed by the might of Heaven.

She stares at me, and for the first time I see fear hidden behind the boldness of her stare. "Stay," she whispers. "Stay forever."

"Yes," I murmur, even though forever means two very different things to each of us. I want the forever she sees from these cliffs where I can lay down my sword and simply be hers.

"Yes," I say, and in that moment, I believe it.

"You don't get to do this, Michael."

Her voice is low and angry, but I hear the tiny quaver hidden behind clenched teeth and sharp words.

"You don't get to come back here after all this time and bring all this back and then die."

Who said anything about dying?

The bitter scents of burning herbs and the sticky resinous perfume of holy oil twist through the room, purifying the air until it tastes of home, the very molecules scoured clean.

If anyone ever kills me, I want it to be you.

"You can't do this to me, Michael," she continues. I pry

my eyes open for a moment and see her head bowed, the curtain of dark hair hiding her face from me. "I was fine. I was helping people. I was fine."

Fine. Humans like that word. I was fine as well. I picked up my sword and carried on as though that perfect golden year hadn't existed.

God's Hand.

God's Sword.

God's Poison.

I was a fool to think I could be anything else.

"Elissa." I try to force my lips to cooperate, but my tongue rests thick in my mouth, and her name comes out as little more than a garbled moan. My body feels foreign, this weakness so strange, so utterly alien that my mind rebels, dragging me back down to a time when I was untouchable.

Phoenicia

53 AD

I take her flying.

Each day, each moment in Elissa's presence is precious to me. I feel her mortality in the back of my mind as low as a heart beating insidiously in my ear, reminding me that each grain of sand that slips through the hourglass is one less second she has left. A year is just a moment to an angel. A century feels like a day.

And in Heaven, she will be different. They always are.

I will be the Archangel, and she will be just another soul.

This fire between us. . . this awakening of feelings I didn't know I was capable of would be snuffed out. Gone.

Impulse was Lucifer's failing, not my own. I have always

been the one who followed the prescribed path, obeying. . . always obeying.

To what reward? The pleasure of slaying my brothers and sisters? Even those that fell to the lowest depths were still my family. Even for all Lucifer's choices, I took no joy in my duty. I take joy in little these days.

Except for Elissa.

So I share with her the one thing that has only ever brought me happiness – the open skies.

I stand at the cliff's edge, far enough from the house that the chances of one of the servants seeing us is slim, though I don't doubt Tanith already suspects I'm something other than human. The old woman is more than willing to turn a blind eye to any of her mistress' peculiarities and that seems to include her choice of lovers.

Lovers.

I know that's what we're barreling toward, and I would be far from the first angel to indulge in such a dalliance. For every dozen angels that look on humanity with thinly veiled disgust, there is one who looks on with curiosity. They feel so much, and it's not surprising that a few of us want to bask in that warmth.

It's only when they abandon their duties in favor of mortal pleasures or bring a Nephilim into being that there are consequences. You can't be surprised to feel your wings scorched when you fly too close to the sun.

The future costs of my decision to stay are nothing but dust and smoke, insubstantial and forgotten a moment later. I have lived untold years, and this is the first time I've allowed myself to want, to need.

If she has bewitched me, so be it.

The wind buffers against my back as I spread my wings, nothing but the empty air behind me.

Elissa's eyes widen, her lips parting as she takes a step

closer, lifting her hand. Her fingers tremble as she draws them down the length of my flight feathers, feeling the power within them. She closes her eyes and breathes deeply, standing frozen a foot from the cliff's edge.

"Your God can create such beauty," she whispers, her voice nearly carried away by the strength of the wind whipping our clothes out like sails. "Why does he allow such ugliness as well?"

"My place is not to question," I reply. The words are automatic, a sentence I've repeated a thousand times as I watched broken humans beg for mercy, for forgiveness, for life. Today, they ring hollow.

Today, I take one more step toward the edge. It's such a long way down.

"Come with me."

Elissa's hand over my wings stills, her eyes meeting mine as she realizes just what I mean. The smile that fills her is like dawn breaking, and she stumbles over her words in her haste to agree.

I curl my forearm under the crook of her legs, lifting her easily. Her arms snake around my shoulder, clenching tight enough to attest to her nervousness. I turn around, standing on the craggy rock, the tips of my toes touching nothing but empty space.

I wait.

Elissa stares out across the water, the view so familiar yet so terrifyingly different with nothing but my arms preventing her from plunging to her death on the rocks a hundred feet below.

Such trust. I pray I never give her reason to regret it.

"Yes."

I take a step forward, out into the empty air, and an updraft catches my wings, pulling us upward. I tighten my arms around Elissa as we take flight.

The sunlight glints off the ocean, the deep turquoise of the waters sparkling like stars so far below us, and in my arms Elissa is laughing. It's the first time I've heard a sound of such pure, untempered joy cross her lips, and I want to hear it again and again.

I dip lower, flying us so close to the surface of the sea that the spray from the waves splashes across our skin. The shoreline fades into a distant blur on the horizon as I tear through the skies.

Elissa's body presses against mine, her heart pounding as I soar higher and higher, scattering a flock of seabirds in a flash of feathers and irritated squawks. Her arms tighten around me as I hover in the air, so far from the safety of land.

"It's so big," she murmurs, her eyes gazing at the distant horizon and places she's only heard about from her trade ships, worlds away from Sidon.

"You can go anywhere. See anything." Her voice trails off as I turn back to shore. "You're free," she adds.

I don't correct her. Free is far from what I am, though I grow closer and closer to forgetting.

When land comes back into her sight she buries her face in my neck. Not from fear. My speed now is far more sedate than earlier as I try to draw out our last moments in flight. Her breath is hot against my neck, and I hear it catch, the familiar cadence growing uneven.

I am not naïve, nor am I a fool.

Some part of me knew where we would end up when I returned here the second time.

I land on the balcony, and before her feet even touch the ground I'm crushing her lips against mine.

There is no hesitation in Elissa, no demure fluttering of eyelashes and feigning of shocked innocence. She has lived outside of man's rules for much of her life, and as I sweep my tongue across her lips, I forget the laws and rules I've been governed by since my creation.

She tastes of honey sweet figs cut with the bitter wine she favors. She is real and human and clinging to me as though she's drowning and only I can save her.

Some part of me wants to laugh at that thought. Elissa has never needed saving. She built her fortress from dust and stones and magic, and even now, even as I have her pressed against the doorway to her study, I'm still amazed she has allowed me entry.

She fumbles with the door, her usual grace fading away as desperation and arousal grows in both of us. The door falls open and she leads me inside, slamming it behind us and shutting out the wind.

With the wind silenced, the quiet of the room is deafening. Elissa's heartbeat pounds against my own, and her bedchamber seems so far away. As if reading my thoughts she pulls me down to the long couch where she sat that very first day, studying her scrolls and dreaming of escape. It seems only fitting that it be here, the afternoon sunlight blazing through the windows, giving us no shadows or subterfuge to hide behind.

I love her.

I break the kiss for a moment, ostensibly to allow her the chance to catch her breath, but in truth, I want nothing but to gaze upon her as I let the realization flow over me.

I'm an angel. My very existence is to serve God's will. I am made to love none but Him and Heaven, and yet here I am, staring down at this woman with her tangled hair and kiss-swollen lips and thinking of only her.

Elissa's brow furrows for a moment, and she sits up, her hair falling back over her shoulders. "Michael," she says, her hand reaching up and pressing against my chest. "Michael, is this what you want?" She hesitates for a moment before adding, "Will you be punished for laying with me?"

I have never lied to her, but some part of me already knows that there will be consequences for both of us. I cannot simply indulge my curiosity in the pleasures of her body and return to Heaven unchanged. But instead I hear my voice say, "No," and her lips are back on mine again.

My hands find the knot of the sash looped around her waist, and I untie it slowly, freeing her from the yards of pale linen encasing her. She sits up again, shrugging out of her robes until she's bare before me. Elissa holds my gaze as she repeats my earlier motions, untying my own belt and pushing my own robes from my shoulders.

We're both as naked as in the Garden, but there is no shame, no shyness or pretense in her face. She smiles slyly as her hand trails over the muscled planes of my chest before dipping lower.

I catch her wrist, unsurprised at her boldness, and pull her onto my lap. She is a tangle of long limbs wrapped around me, her bronzed skin nearly humming in breathless excitement. I fell her core pressed against me, molten heat anointing me, and the desperate need I feel nearly overwhelms me. I want nothing more than to thrust upward and bury myself in her heat, to finally put an end to this dance we've been circling in since the day we met. Yet still I hold myself in check.

"You couldn't have thought I would just lay on my back and let myself be taken, Archangel Michael." Her words are teasing, forcing me out of my own head, and I kiss my way down her neck, nipping at the pulse that flutters beneath my lips.

"We'll see who ends up being taken," I murmur against her skin. I run my fingertips across the curve of her breast, smiling as she shivers, her nipples tightening into hard peaks beneath my touch.

Her ankles lock behind my back, and we are pressed skin against skin, her breasts crushed against my chest, her face buried in my neck. She shifts her hips and chokes on a gasp as I breach her. Warm, wet heat surrounds me as she sinks down, and my fingers dig into the softness of her hips, hard enough to leave bruises.

Elissa lifts her head from the crook of my neck and just stares at me, those pale eyes wider than I've ever seen them.

"My Archangel," she purrs, rocking her hips against mine.

I capture her mouth in another kiss, silencing her words. I have no desire to be the Archangel in this moment. The weight of my wings against my back and my blades at my side are forgotten. I want nothing to exist beyond the confines of this bright room and the sweet spaces of her body.

If this is the scope of human love, I cease to wonder how wars can erupt for the sake of it.

I push Elissa backward so that she's reclining on the couch, and for all her earlier protestations that she was not one to lay back and be taken I hear no complaints. She hooks one long leg around my thigh, driving me deeper into her.

I hold myself up, the muscles in my forearms straining, but it's worth it to gaze down at Elissa, a deep flush coloring her skin. Sweat beads in the hollow of her throat, the room already growing hot with the doors and windows shut tight against the wind. I follow the path of one tiny drop as it slips downward between her breasts.

Her restless hands claw into my back, hard enough that I'd be bleeding if I were human, and I reach up and take one hand in mine, drawing it down over my shoulder to press against her own peaked nipple. She inhales sharply at her own touch, and I feel her tighten around me in pleasure. I duck my head, drawing my tongue over her other nipple, relishing as the volume of her moans grows.

Her other hand flexes against my shoulder blade, five

points of pressure digging into my flesh. Elissa surrounds me, the scent of her skin, the heat of her touch. Her head is thrown back, pressing into the cushions as she rocks against me, the rhythm as primal as the tides.

Her eyes are closed as she loses herself in pure sensation, and in that moment I want them to open. I want to see each part of her, but even more, I want her to see me.

"Open your eyes." I hardly recognize my voice. The command that soaks every word is gone, discarded somewhere on the floor along with my robes. I sound broken, my vocal cords blown out and strained with my quickly slipping control.

She opens her eyes - the palest blue of the highest skies, that point where Earth meets Heaven.

And she smiles, all teasing gone. The pink tip of her tongue wets her lips as she gasps when I snap my hips forward. The delicious pressure builds, heat that could boil the seas outside our door, and it's Elissa that breaks first. A cry that is partially my name, partially a pure, wild noise of bliss tears from her throat. If the rest of the household had any doubts about us, they're certainly gone now.

Elissa clings to me as she shudders around me, and it's nearly too much. I feel human, feel the blood pounding through my body, the sweet slick warmth between her thighs, the burning aching of my own pleasure rising to meet hers, and it's glorious and terrifying all at once.

I bury my face in her neck, whispering words of worship and love in the language of creation, etching them into her very skin as the last thread of my control snaps and I spill within her. My wings fight to break free, but I will them back.

Let us both forget what I am, just for a moment.

As we lay in the circle of each other's arms, our heartbeats calming and gasps giving way to even breaths, there are no constant angelic battles vying for my attention, there is no

Father demanding my obedience. In this moment, my touch is not poison.

The thoughts are blasphemy, but today, I welcome them.

Cocooned in the warmth of the room there is only she and I. And it is enough.

7
ELISSA

I sit beside Caila's bed, watching as Michael tosses and turns as the toxin eats its way through his system. The blankets are a tangled froth of white and pink around him, the fluffy pillows and delicate fabrics looking out of place around his muscular body.

Sweat beads on his chest, soaking through the bandage Grace hastily taped over the wound, and his hands shift restlessly on the covers, his fingers clenching and unclenching on the fabric. I've never seen Michael look so vulnerable. . . so human. His brow furrows, and his eyes dart back and forth beneath his eyelids.

Do angels dream? I lean forward, brushing my fingertips across his brow, the skin clammy as his body fights off what infects him. There were so many things I never asked.

A year. One bright, beautiful year out of two thousand. After so much time, memories start to blur. The names and faces of the background players in my life recede into hazy recollections, but every day, every minute of that year still stands out in glorious Technicolor as the only period in my life where I was truly happy.

Just happy.

I wasn't desperately striving for something I didn't really believe I could attain, carving out a fortress on the edge of the world to protect my heart.

One single year. And somehow even after I've watched the world I grew up in disappear into the ocean, and we've both seen a dozen other empires rise and fall, we can't move on.

It feels inevitable that one day we would end up back here.

The jaded broken part of me whispers that this wasn't supposed to happen.

I was supposed to rip out the offending arrow and wait for the Archangel constitution to heal him while the four of us plotted and planned how to break Caila out of this prison. I'd sit across from him, cold and unforgiving, as we worked. I'd make him suffer and regret.

I'd make him feel weak.

But I'd be the bigger person and put my antagonism on hold. We'd tear through the wards, our collective power no match for the vicious witch in her mansion, and once the battle was won, Michael would fly off back to Heaven once again. My life would return to what it had been for so long, and he would slip back into memories and dreams.

Instead, I sit in the dark, perched on an overstuffed ottoman at the edge of the bed. The weak yellow light of the one grimy streetlight still working filters in through the blinds, and I count his shallow breaths and hold my own as I wait for his eyelids to flicker open.

Lucifer hovers in the doorway, and I've never understood him more than tonight in this darkened house. His seething hatred for his brother's crimes against him bonded us so long ago. Grace tempers that boiling rage, but he doesn't know how to reconcile century upon century of despising Michael with this abrupt reminder of the elder brother he once loved.

Join the club.

His footsteps recede away from me, and a moment later the back door slams. I can't blame him for that. I spent more years than I can count running away.

"So. You and Michael."

Grace doesn't skirt around the elephant in the room, doesn't couch her questions in subtleties because she's afraid of offending me. I appreciate it. When dawn breaks, I don't doubt I'll be back to my old self, burying anything real under an armor of black leather and deflection, but not tonight.

Tonight, I indulge myself and brush my fingertips across his forehead and remember.

"Yeah. Me and Michael."

Grace sits down on the ottoman next to me. It's too small to accommodate us both comfortably, so I move to the edge of the bed, close enough that I can feel the heat radiating from Michael as he restlessly shifts. She has a white coffee mug in her hand, and she offers it to me.

"Tea?" I ask.

"Bourbon."

I chuckle. "Girl after my own heart. Give it here." I take a hearty sip of the liquor, barely noticing the burn. I'm just glad for anything to wash out the taste of copper and rot that still clings to my tongue hours later.

A pile of plaster and dust rests on the floor beside the wardrobe, nothing more than a mound in the darkness, but before I dared bring Michael in here, I jammed my knife into the wall, cutting apart the sigil until half the wall lay crumbled at my feet.

I know I should clean it up, sweep the last remnants of that poisoned blood out of here, but I can't bring myself to move. Not yet.

Grace waits, that same unnerving stillness that Michael had when he was trying to puzzle something out. And just like back then, I'm the mystery.

"Granted, I've only met four angels," she says, "And one was trying to kill me and the other two were Fallen, but Michael just didn't strike me as the type to-" Grace's voice trails off as she tries to search for the polite way to describe my broken relationship.

"The type to toy with a human?"

Grace shakes her head, her golden curls hiding her face for a moment before she raises her head, politeness and pretense quickly put aside. "To fall in love." I scoff, but Grace ignores me as she soldiers on. "Look, I don't know any of the history between the three of you. Lucifer wouldn't say anything except that it's your story to tell or not tell, but I do have eyes."

Michael groans as he turns on the bed, and one of his hands twitches, a graceless spasm that looks so wrong on him that I'm reaching across his body and clasping his hand before I can stop myself.

So much for cold detachment there, Elissa.

"He was different," I say, forcing myself to look away from him and turn to Grace. I take another sip of the bourbon, the ice cubes clinking softly against the ceramic of the mug. "I was young. The whole world was young. Of course, I haven't had much time to judge who he is now. Lucifer certainly has changed."

"What happened?"

I want to brush her off, to ignore the query that threatens to bring back the one memory I desperately want to avoid reliving.

My voice is clipped when I reply, "Heaven forced him to make a choice. He didn't choose me."

8
MICHAEL

Awakening is like clawing through the surface of water blackened with an oil slick. The enveloping darkness calls me back, the sweet thrall of my memories beckoning me to bury myself in their depths, and I want so badly to give in.

Instead, I choke on the brackish water and come out the other side wheezing for air. I sit up, the sweaty blankets falling away as a wave of dizziness momentarily whites out my vision. The plastic of a bandage crinkles as I roll my shoulder. I rip it off, staring down at the small red circle next to my heart that nearly killed me.

That would have killed me if Elissa hadn't been there.

Elissa. . . my memories of the last few hours are hazy at best, but I know I didn't imagine her fingertips on my brow and her low voice alternately begging me not to die and cursing me for existing in the first place.

Phoenicia
54 AD

THE FAMILIAR PULL of Heaven calling me back intensifies. Once, I would have found it comforting, that sound in the back of my mind reminding me of home, the collective voices of my brothers and sisters coalescing into a hum that rises higher and higher until I obey.

If I concentrate on a single voice the words become clear. "Michael, you are summoned." Over and over again, repeated in a thousand voices.

In all my years of life, I've never ignored a summons. Even in the midst of battle, if I've been called back, I obeyed instantly. Even bloodied and battered after the fight with Lucifer, I spread my damaged wings and made my way home as quickly as my injured body was able.

The summons jolts me to awareness as I lay dozing in Elissa's bed, tangled in soft linens. Elissa sleeps beside me, the bare expanse of her back tempting me to stay.

Would it be so terrible if I did? Would the world notice?

I ignore the call, pulling the soft sheets over us both and forgetting myself in the taste of her skin.

It works for a day.

Heaven will not be ignored, and the call grows louder, the pitch increasing, building upon itself, layer after layer of sound rising in volume until it drowns out my thoughts, until my vision blurs as my brain shudders under the endless, unceasing din.

I slip away as Elissa rests, telling myself that I'll return before she wakes. There's no need to worry her over nothing. Metatron is flexing his wings as always, taking his usual petty joy in reminding me that while I might be God's fists, only he is God's voice.

The shrieking tone of the summons softens the closer my

wings take me to Heaven, the piercing timbre sliding back into the calming voices of my brothers and sisters. The moment I pass through the gates I wonder for the briefest moment why I would ever want to leave again.

But a beautiful cage is still a cage.

Metatron waits, impatience painted across his blandly serene countenance. While the Archangels and lower angels look as varied and unique as the humans on the Earth, Metatron has always been a blank slate, a doughy face with undefined features always watching. He follows my movements with those watery blue eyes, his face so unremarkable that alone makes it unique.

Before Father fell silent to all but him, Metatron was merely the scribe. A recording device to make certain the words were never lost. But he was not an Archangel. We stood apart, first in Father's eyes until Lucifer who wore his pride like a mantle shattered that.

As we five splintered, Metatron rose. And behind that flat, empty stare, I know he remembers how we once kept him at a distance.

Metatron waits for me far from the heavy silence of the central chamber. He rarely leaves it anymore. The throne room. It has never been called by another name, though each year that passes removes it further from the space when my Father sat beside us. It feels like a tomb now, the sheer walls of marble polished to a silver sheen rising far above our heads until they disappear into the skies. The throne sits empty, the unadorned stone smooth as water and just as cold.

And there Metatron waits in this sterile chamber, day after day, year after year, an empty vessel awaiting His voice.

Except for today. Today Metatron stands just inside the gates, a placid smile across his lips that looks jarringly out of place on him.

"Michael," he says, dipping his head in greeting. "You are late. That is unlike you."

I refuse to rise to the bait, remembering that same smile the day I was ordered to raise my blade against Lucifer. "Apologies, brother," I reply. "I was detained."

"I'm aware of just what has detained you, Michael."

I hear the threat in his voice and every part of me goes tense and wary. Metatron notices.

Of course he does. With centuries of nothing to do but watch us all, he misses nothing.

"Walk with me, Michael." I follow at his heels, wondering not for the first time why of all of us Metatron was the last one my Father chose to speak to. Metatron walks seemingly without aim, and I seethe in the silence. He is nothing if not patient though, and soon I find myself desperately awaiting his oily voice, even if it's to give me another order.

He is God's voice, after all, while I'm nothing but God's blunt instrument.

"She's quite lovely, Michael. For a human." He breaks the silence without warning, and I stop abruptly. The gates to the Garden loom ahead, though Uriel is absent from his post, no doubt wandering through the depths, losing a bit more of himself among the flowers each day.

"She's of no consequence," I reply quickly. "Merely a diversion."

"A diversion," Metatron echoes. "A diversion that leads you to ignore your orders?" The deceptively light tone of his voice drops away and his next words are flinty, "You forget your place, Archangel."

I draw myself up to my full height, head and shoulders above Metatron's diminutive form. It is not arrogance speaking when I say I know I'm much more formidable than he. Metatron has never raised a sword in the celestial battles, never held the life of another angel in his hand, never been anything but a jealous mouthpiece for one greater than himself.

And he laughs.

There are none on Earth and few in Heaven or Hell that would dare challenge me. Metatron knows I could crush him before he could stop me, but still he laughs.

He laughs because he knows my hands are tied. Lucifer's insurrection is still too fresh, too raw. An attack on him would be seen as an attack on Heaven itself, and I would be unaided. No one would side with me against the throne.

And Metatron knows it.

I back down, hating him just a bit more for the self-satisfied smirk that grows on his lips.

"My orders," I grind out, "were to discover what the witch's motives are, and if she poses a danger to Heaven. I've done that."

"You certainly have." My eyes flash, and I clench my jaw tighter in an effort to keep silent. "Always such a hothead, Michael," he drawls, walking closer to the border of the Garden. He narrows his eyes at the unattended gate. "You aren't the only Archangel neglecting his duties as of late. Seems as though Lucifer is the only one to actually follow through on his words."

Metatron strides through the gate, leaving me gaping at his back. Lucifer's name is barely spoken in Heaven, and when he is mentioned it's in low, hushed voices as though invoking his name will bring the devil's wrath down upon any angel unwary enough to use it. It certainly isn't thrown around casually as an example of angelic efficiency.

I enter the Garden, expecting to see Metatron hovering just inside the gates but instead he's ambling down one of the many paths to pause in front of a patch of gladiolus, their spiky red blooms pointed to the sky. He plucks one from the soil, turning the large flower over in his hand before speaking.

"The humans have taken to calling this one the sword lily," he says, tugging one crimson petal free from the stem. "I rather like it." He squeezes the petal between his thumb and forefinger, the delicate blossom bruising under his touch. "It is so breakable though." He tosses the ruined stem down onto the soil. "All of our Father's creations are so breakable."

Metatron turns to me, all traces of subtlety gone. "I could order you to kill her, you know," he states, his voice flat as though he was just discussing another flower. "What would you do then?" He takes a step closer, his eyes never leaving mine as he appraises my reaction. "Would you fall? Sever your wings for the love of one of them?"

"Are these your words or Father's?" I snap, tiring of Metatron's mind games.

He ignores my question as he continues. "She has already made herself an enemy of Heaven by tempting an Archangel to fall."

He's right. However Metatron might be twisting Heaven's laws to suit his own whims, I know how Elissa will be seen by my brothers and sisters.

As an enemy, a creature of darkness and evil, bending the will of the mighty Michael to her base, human desires. Metatron may be unwilling to sully his own hands with her blood, but dozens would. Thrones and Dominions eager to curry favor amongst those that outrank them, Powers and Principalities seeing it as their duty to free me from her thrall.

Metatron need only say the word.

I nod my head stiffly as understanding grows in me. Metatron rests his hand on my shoulder, murmuring words of approval like perfumed poison in my ear. "I knew you were more than just an executioner, Michael," he says, his fingers tightening, digging into muscle and bone. "There will be talk, of course, but all this unpleasantness will be forgotten soon enough."

I numbly allow myself to be steered along the path, the plants and flowers nothing but a bright blur in my peripheral vision. Metatron stops, and I nearly trip over him, my body on autopilot as my mind runs in circles, trying to think of an escape from the fate I see looming before me.

"You've made the right choice, Michael. For once."

"Leave me." My voice sounds choked to my own ears, the words a plea rather than the order I wish them to be.

For the first time in all the years I've known him, Metatron holds his tongue. I barely notice as he leaves, his absence failing to offer the solace I hoped for.

It's over. That much is sure.

The thick perfume of the Garden turns oppressive, the cloying nectar of a thousand blooms blocking my throat. I rush along the path and burst through the gates and take to the skies.

I fly at breakneck speed, trying to outpace the truth or at least find a place to suffer in silence.

Heaven has its own borders, and I find my way there, alighting on the edge of a cliff, the sheer precipice so achingly familiar, though instead of the glinting blue of the ocean below there is only a featureless black void.

I'm not surprised my wings took me here.

The rocks bear the scars of our blades, the pale stone still stained with blood and broken feathers, his and my own. Heaven has no rain to wash it away, no wind to blow the evidence into the void that leads to Hell.

It's here where I fought Lucifer, on these rocks where we beat each other bloody, shattering teeth and bones, spraying the stones with each other's blood like a gruesome fountain. I stand at the edge, staring down into nothingness at the place I snapped my brother's wings and pushed him over the edge.

For what?

I could fall. Sever my own wings and my connection to

Heaven and live as a human, hidden away in her villa at the edge of the world. I see Elissa, see the joy on her face even as time passes and streaks of silver cut through her dark hair. I see myself laying down my sword, lines growing on my face like dried riverbeds, my back growing stooped and weak. I see the years piling up like bricks, time truly meaning something when it's no longer infinite.

It's a beautiful dream.

Were I just another angel, it might be possible. I would become a cautionary tale passed through the garrison. "Be careful among the humans. Don't allow yourself to grow too close, too attached, or you might end up like him." They would stop speaking my name, as though my choice to fall was some disease they could contract.

But I'm not just another angel. I'm Michael, and my hands have never been my own. I was a fool to think otherwise.

I stare out at the void, standing in the very spot Lucifer stood awaiting me before that final battle.

And I understand.

"I'm sorry, brother," I whisper to the empty air.

SHE IS in her study when I return. One of the trade ships arrived in Sidon three days ago, laden with gold and ivory from the eastern routes, and her head has been buried in ledgers and scrolls since then.

For the first time, I wish that I could keep myself cloaked from her. I want just a few moments to watch her before I have to do this.

"Michael!"

Elissa springs from her seat, figures and records forgotten, and she's in my arms. Her lips are on mine, her mouth parting as her hands sweep across my back. She smells of incense and fire, of magic and life, and I want so much to forget the last day, to bundle her onto one of her ships and take her across the world.

I allow myself that momentary dream of losing ourselves in Egypt or Rome and letting the crowds swallow us up. But there's no hiding from Heaven. Not for me, and not for her as long as she's by my side.

Elissa pulls back, sensing the change in me. She cocks her head to the side, her eyes narrowing as she takes me in.

She would want to fight. Elissa has never given up easily. She carved a life for herself from bare stone and the strength of her will, harnessing powers in a few short years that normally take a lifetime to master.

She will fight back, and she will lose.

They will make an example of her, just a broken thing to be held up as an effigy against defying the will of Heaven. I look at her, at the warmth of her soul glowing bright as the midday sun when she looks at me, and I know this is my punishment.

I never questioned the decree from Father that ordered me to be my brother's executioner. It didn't matter that my orders were to stop just before the killing blow, the brother I loved still died that day.

If this was a test, I failed.

I deserve her hatred.

"I've been called back," I say. My voice sounds as though it's coming from miles away.

"Called back?" she repeats, her brow furrowing. "But you're not going, are you?" I stay silent, biting the inside of my cheek raw as I fight to keep my face neutral. "Michael," she says again, her voice growing louder, sharper. "Michael, you're not going back?"

She closes her mouth as the realization washes over her, and it's as though the light in her eyes, that glorious, joyous brightness that surrounds her is snuffed out in an instant. Despite myself, I take a step closer to her and she immediately recoils.

"I'm sorry," I say, knowing my words ring hollow. "I have my duties to consider."

She laughs, and it sounds nothing like the elation as we flew through the skies. "Your duties. Was this something you were ordered to do?" Her voice breaks, but her eyes are dry. "Was I just a duty?"

"Never." The word slips out of me before I can stop it, and I'm so close to telling her that it was all a mistake, but I see Metatron's smirking face and hear the crack of the bones in Lucifer's wings.

God's Hands.

God's Broken, Bloody Fists.

God's Poison.

"I enjoyed our time together, but this place is not my home. It never was." I steel myself, drawing on the cold, dead part of me that allowed me to drive a sword into my brother's flesh and say the words I know will end us. "My duty to Heaven is something you can never understand."

Something flickers in her eyes for the barest moment. The same shocked betrayal Lucifer wore in that instant before I pushed him into the Pit. Then her pale eyes turn cold as she draws her anger around her like a shroud.

"Get out." Her voice is clipped, as she stands still in the center of the room. She's still close enough to touch, and she lifts her chin, staring defiantly at me, unwilling to cede even a single step to me in her own home.

"Leave," she says, her voice never wavering.

And I do.

9

ELISSA

"You're alive then."

The fire crackles, the flames rising higher than the meager scraps of kindling piled in the rusted firepit should allow. Wasting any of my energy right now is foolish, but the slightly too red color of the conjured flames comforts me. It's the first spell I truly mastered. I sit on the cracked cement steps and stare into the flames.

For the first time in a long time, I'm not looking for anything in the serpentine motion of the fire.

"Seems like it."

Michael's voice is rough, as though he spent the last few hours yelling instead of comatose in Caila's bed, but I don't turn around. I don't look at him.

He hovers behind me, his presence threatening to tug me closer like it always has, the magnetic pull that neither of us has ever been able to deny.

Until he did.

"Why are you here, Michael? Really."

He squeezes past me on the narrow stairs and steps

between me and the fire, blocking my view and forcing me to look at him.

His chest is bare, the bloody mess of his shirt still somewhere on the floor beside the bed. The quarter sized wound that nearly ended him is little more than a red indentation on his skin now. In a few more hours, all traces of his ordeal will be gone, his angelic body erasing any evidence of the injury.

My eyes rake across the chiseled planes of Michael's muscles, remembering running my fingers across that warrior's body and feeling him shudder beneath me. I poured wine down his chest once, licking the sticky sweet liquid away where it pooled and tracing the contours of his abs with the tip of my tongue before dipping my head even lower and giving him a real taste of Heaven.

Those days are long past, and I quiet the hunger that always sprung in me when we were close. Unaware of my inner thoughts, Michael's face wears that same earnest, painfully honest expression he wore while whispering words of forever in my ears. "I wasn't lying when I said I was sent here."

"For what purpose? Has Heaven taken another *interest* in me?" I can't help the snide tone. After all, Heavenly orders were what threw Michael into my life the first time.

Michael shakes his head. "Grace. Lucifer." He sighs, leaning heavily against the rough wooden railing that borders both sides of the staircase. "Raphael believes there will be retaliation from some of the angels for Uriel. If something happens to Grace, and Heaven is behind it. . ."

"Lucifer will burn Heaven to the ground," I finish.

Michael nods gravely. "I'm here to make sure he never has a reason to." Michael has that same apologetic, kicked puppy look when he continues, "I didn't know you were here. I would have left you alone."

"You're good at that, aren't you?" Before Michael can protest, I add, "I almost want to hate her, you know. I wish I could hate her." At Michael's confused look, I clarify, "Grace. But you can't hate her. She's good. She's kind. She's a much better person than I am, and then there's the two of them together."

I close my eyes, willing away the memories of being looked at like that. "It's almost sickening how happy they are." My voice softens, the sharp edges blunting. "He looks at her when she's not paying attention. Even though I've barely spent more than a few hours with them, you can't help noticing it. Lucifer looks at her with this awe, as though he doesn't have any regrets about falling now because *she* is his Heaven. So yes, I wish I could hate her for it."

I chuckle to myself. You know you have problems when you look to the devil as an example of a healthy relationship. I flick my wrist and the fire flares a bit brighter, the flames licking the edge of the pit as they fight over the last scraps of fuel, the growing light at his back plunging Michael into silhouette.

Almost as an afterthought, I add, "But then, she is one of you after all. Even before she came into herself the Last was never just another human."

"Neither were you."

"That's rich."

"That's true," he counters.

I glare up at Michael, the ire I worked so hard to control in his presence growing as the flames at his back lick higher. "I was your beach vacation and a warm body to lose yourself in while you worked through your Daddy issues." Michael takes a step closer, his face still hidden in shadow, his eyes unreadable.

"I was never more than just another human to you. You fed me pretty lies of choosing me over Heaven, but that's all they were. As soon as Daddy snapped his celestial fingers you ran back to Heaven. And I'm sure you weren't the first angel to whisper words of love to some shepherd's daughter to pry apart her knees."

Before I can blink, Michael is up the two short steps and standing over me, grabbing my shoulders and hauling me to my feet. He stands on the step below me and now that we're eye to eye I can see the blazing anger in his face.

"Don't do that," he spits. "Don't cheapen it."

I shove him back, and he's still off balance enough that he ends up in an undignified heap in the grass.

"Don't touch me." I can still feel his hands gripping my skin, his touch branding me the way it always did. "You don't get to decide how I feel, Michael. And if I want to cheapen our great love to an Archangel deciding to screw a human to see what all the fuss is about, you can't stop me."

Michael raises himself up on his elbows, but makes no effort to get up from where he's sprawled on the grass. "But then, I guess I should be thanking you." I slowly make my way down the steps, walking around Michael to stand by the fire. It's nearly six feet tall now, fed with spite and fury, all the fuel long since burned away. I cup my palm, cutting it through the air and the flames drop down to a more manageable height. I turn back to Michael as he stands up. "If you had actually cared enough to stay, we might have had a beautiful life together," I say, "but I'd be nothing but dust and bones by now."

"I made a mistake."

"No, I did." Michael flinches, and the fact that his suffering brings me no joy makes me even angrier at myself. I barely know who I'm speaking to when I continue.

"I thought I knew what it was to hate. I thought I hated my sisters and my mother for looking at me like I was some filthy dog that wandered into their house that they were expected to feed," I whisper. "I thought I knew what hate was when my father tried to sell me to the brothel for a handful of coins and few cups of wine."

"I'm sor-"

"Don't," I interrupt. "Don't tell me that you're sorry or that you have regrets. Don't do that to me." The silence stretches out between us, and I make no move to fill it.

"The girl you knew did die, and she died hating you. Leave the dead buried."

Phoenicia

54 AD

Dust and ashes.

Blood and bone.

He's gone. He's really gone. He's left me, and-

No.

I silence the rising tide of grief that threatens to pull me under, the choking, drowning waves that turn every bright memory into poison.

I will not be another wailing woman, gnashing my teeth and rending my clothes as I weep at the injustice of love.

I learned long ago that the only justice that exists is what I create with my own hands. I lost sight of that in his arms.

I won't forget again.

I burst through the doorway into the kitchen. Tanith is twisting a plait into Sisa's dark hair, murmuring sweet words into the child's ear as her gnarled fingers weave the glossy black strands into a wreath of intricate waves fit for a fine lady.

Their cheerful greetings fall on deaf ears as I drop to my knees in front of the cold fireplace, scooping up ashes and cinders with my bare hands.

"Mistress?" Tanith's crackling voice is hesitant, and I stare down into the hearth, to my grey streaked hands, schooling my features before I stand up, the ashes cupped carefully in my palm.

"It's fine," I reply. I pause in the doorway before adding. "Don't enter my study tonight."

I fill the gleaming brass bowl that Amma passed down to me with the ashes, and I barely feel the cut as I slash the blade through my palm. The blood drips down, the rivulets of red turning dusty grey as it mixes. I draw my fingers through the mixture, sticky and dry, and I walk outside.

The wind is never silent here on the edge of the cliffs. It roars through my ears, snapping my hair over my shoulders. I draw my fingers across the bleached white stone of the wall, painting the sigil that will bar him from entering. I press my still bleeding palm to the center and feel the ward wrap around the house, cloaking it from Heaven's prying eyes.

I can feel the darkness descend around the house as surely as the sun slipping behind a cloud.

But there will be no break in the storm today.

I step back inside, yanking the shutters closed behind me and plunging the room into murky half-light.

I lose track of the hours. They slip together in the dim room, the shadows growing deeper as dusk crawls into night, and still I sit, staring at the darkened corner where he first appeared to me.

My hand aches, and my nose is filled with the bitter tang of blood and ashes.

The moon is high when I stand up on stiff legs and push open the door. The wind has quieted, the air still for the first time in months. The sigil stares back at me, blood and ash looking black in the moonlight. I feel the twinge in my palm as the magic flowing through it pulses around me.

I reach up and draw my nails through the markings,

breaking the lines. I feel the ward snap instantly. I leave the door gaping open as I walk back inside.

I wait.

Dawn breaks around me, the black of the night sky fading into purple before erupting with streaks of pink and orange as the sun crests the horizon. The morning glides into another beautiful day, the cloudless skies the brightest shade of blue.

Sounds from the household filter through the walls, the murmur of feminine voices that always brought me comfort fading into white noise as I wait.

Dusk has fallen again and the last rays of the sun have dyed the ocean the color of blood when I hear the sound of wings.

The dying light frames his silhouette as he stands in the doorway, but I don't need light to see that the angel is not Michael.

He steps over my threshold, his wings trailing behind him, the feathers black as pitch. While Michael's presence always made me feel lighter, some part of his angelic nature easing the burden of my soul with his mere presence, I feel nothing but dark anger pouring from him.

I should be afraid, but I know that anger isn't meant for me.

"Elissa," he says, and his voice is like silk.

"Who are you?" I ask. "Come into the light."

The unlit torches and oil lamps in the room all flare to life at once, the sudden brightness jarring. I blink for a moment as my eyes adjust.

He stands unmoving, watching my reaction impassively. He is Michael's opposite in every way. Inky black robes swirl around him, and his hair and eyes are as dark as his wings. When he takes another step closer to me he moves like a predator, like the beasts shipped into Rome for the gladiator fights, violent energy coiled in his muscles just waiting for the moment to strike.

"I am called Lucifer," he replies. He's standing right in front of me, gazing down at where I've sat frozen for the last day. He extends a hand to me, and I hesitate. "Heaven tried to make me kneel once. It's done the same to you, I see."

Bristling, I rise unaided, and Lucifer smiles. "I see what drew him to you, but I see so much more." Lucifer takes a step closer until he's near enough that I can feel the heat radiating off his body and smell the scent of smoke and spice clinging to his skin.

One hand reaches up and brushes a lock of my hair from my face, and I lift up my chin, staring unflinchingly at him.

"Such spirit was wasted on my brother." I can't hide the flinch that goes through me as he mentions Michael. Lucifer sees it.

"Michael wronged us both. The sound of your soul screaming hatred for Heaven echoed into the depths of Hell." Lucifer takes one of my limp hands in his and draws me into the center of the room. The heat from the flames and burning oil in the lamps in the still air of the room grows stifling but he shows no discomfort even as the flames dance across his face.

I have wondered if all angels were as beautiful as Michael, and I have my answer.

Lucifer circles me slowly, appraising me like a beast at auction. I know the barest story of who he is. I pried many tales of his people from Michael in the past year, and Lucifer's fate was the one account Michael skimmed over.

As though reading my thoughts, Lucifer asks, "What has your beloved Michael told you of me?"

"You are an angel who defied God and started a war in Heaven. You lost, and as punishment you were banished to Hell," I parrot Michael's words.

Lucifer's lips curl into a sneer of disgust. "I'm not surprised that's what you were told. History is written by the winners, after all," he spits. He ceases his endless circuit around me, standing by my side, but still so close.

"Heaven likes compliance. Deference. Blind obedience." I turn my head to watch him as he speaks, and I know his words are the truth. "That's why my dear brother is one of Heaven's most favored sons, and our Father ordered him to cut me down." The bitterness that drips from his voice is so familiar.

"You loved him," I state.

"Yes," Lucifer replies without hesitating. "And he made his choice."

I drop my eyes to the ground for a moment, emotions swirling through me, love and lust, pain and betrayal, all wrapped up in the image of Michael's face.

Heaven made the demands, but Michael chose to obey them.

I lift my head back up, staring into the darkness of Lucifer's eyes, and his lips curl up into a smile as he reads the resolve in me.

"I think we can make a deal."

There are many paths to power. All require discipline and study, but I shied away from the darkest magics. I was able to harness the wild magic of the land and sea, and they demanded tribute in blood and bone and pain, but it was always mine. I did not toy with the lives of others or traffic in the dead. I crawled to the edge of the cliff, but I never jumped.

But like Lucifer, I was pushed.

"A deal?" I echo. "For my soul?"

Lucifer chuckles as he shakes his head. "Your soul can't be bought or sold. It doesn't work that way. I thought to barter for your place in Heaven, but now I see what you truly were to him. Consider this a gift."

His hands brush over my bare arms, and I can't hide the flush of desire that fills me at his touch. Lucifer's lips brush the shell of my ear, and his voice is barely above a whisper when he speaks again. "The place you have in his heart is far more valuable to me than the place you have in Heaven."

I feel the wash of power flood me at that touch, feel fire tear through my veins as the devil remakes me in the flickering candlelight, burning away my mortality, scorching my soul black as his wings.

It's overwhelming, pain and pleasure twisting and coiling over each other until I've lost the sense entirely of which sensation is which. Somewhere in that deep void I've fallen into, I hear Lucifer's voice in my ear, his low words like a caress. "We are the same, you and I. The ones betrayed and cast aside. Never again."

I feel my own power growing, my skin stretching too tight as the magic I harnessed on my own flexes and expands, doubling and redoubling until I'm nearly blinded by the intensity of it all.

My knees buckle, and Lucifer catches me, lowering me to the floor with a surprising gentleness. Already I can feel the dizziness receding as the shattered pieces of my mortal self knit back together into something new. Something better.

Let Michael have his subservience. I didn't tear free of the stranglehold of man's rules to be bound by Heaven's.

He made his choice, and I made mine.

MICHAEL'S HAND brushes my arm, and that simple touch is like throwing a match into a bucket of gasoline. The air between us thickens, and it has nothing to do with the perpetual Louisiana humidity and everything to do with the way Michael stares at me in the firelight. His pupils are wide, deep blue swallowed up by blackness, and he looks like a starving man staring at a feast.

I remember being the focus of that stare, that unwavering angelic attention. It was intoxicating then, and after so many years of living without or passing my nights with forgettable trysts that mean nothing beyond tactile comfort, I want to be devoured again.

I take a step closer, all thoughts of personal space gone. Michael's breath is labored and heavy, and I reach upward and press my fingers against the fading wound on his chest, the softest touch. I feel a shudder go through him.

"Elissa," he breathes. Twenty centuries later, and he still says my name the same way, drawing it out slowly, breathing the sibilance of the word out on a languid exhale, as though he's savoring the taste of it on his tongue.

I hate him, and I love him, and most of all I miss him. I miss the sunlight streaming into my study as Michael told me of the lands he'd seen, the places he had been. I miss watching the weariness drop away from his face as weeks slipped into months, and his secret jokes with Tanith, and the trinkets he would bring for Sisa. I miss the taste of his skin and the warmth of his mouth.

Our lips meet and there's nothing gentle about this kiss. Our teeth clash together, lips bruising as we both vie for dominance, neither one willing to cede to the other after so long.

I'm not surprised that Michael can still play my body like no other. His grip on my arm tightens as he pulls me even closer, and I slam the door on the ugly memory of that last day. I forget the taste of blood and ashes and regret and only remember the years without him, aching for him, for this.

We fit together the way we always did – each of us a bent

and mangled key that fits only in one matching lock. When Michael pulls back from the kiss and I take that second to gulp down oxygen, I see the question of *what now?* in his eyes and choose to ignore it.

Dawn will be breaking too soon, putting an end to this maddening, terrifying night. Tomorrow I will regret this, I'm sure, but for these last few hours of darkness I want to burn his touch into my memory.

The fire still glows a few feet away, the embers pulsing in time with our synced heartbeats, and I wonder if the flames will continue to rise unchecked, spilling out of the pit to catch the grass around us, scorching the land until only blackened dust is left.

Seems a fitting enough metaphor.

I shiver as I feel his lips over my pulse, his teeth scraping my jugular, and a noise rips from my throat, a needy whine that would embarrass me any other time. Tonight though, it only incenses Michael more as he nips and licks his way up my throat before pressing a kiss to my bottom lip, meeting my gasp with his own desperate groan.

His hands ghost over my arms, so close but not quite touching, and I bite down on his lip, just hard enough to say without words, *I won't break*.

Not again.

I hook my foot around his calf, urging him to the ground. Michael arches an eyebrow at my choice but doesn't speak. We're both too afraid to let words shatter the spell between us. The grass is cool under my hands as Michael hauls me onto his lap, his hands fisting my shirt, stretching the worn cotton of my tank top as he tries to get closer.

The long shadows of the flickering flames make it easy to forget how exposed we really are, but it could be blazing daylight and I still wouldn't care about anything but getting closer. I feel Michael hard against my inner thigh, feel his hips shifting underneath me as he fights to hold himself in check, and I peel my shirt over my head, tossing it along with my bra aside into the darkness.

Michael's hands are on my skin in an instant, fusing his touch into me as his fingers trace my spine, each vertebra another space to relearn. His other hand curls around my waist, crushing me against his chest, skin to skin, flesh to flesh, and I'm not sure if the harsh, panting breaths are from his throat or mine.

I rock against him, and despite the fact that I threw aside cumbersome gowns and dresses the moment it became remotely acceptable in society, I silently curse whoever invented pants. Too many layers of fabric still separate us, and I'm not yet willing to leave the circle of his arms, even for a moment.

My hand is splayed out across Michael's side, and I drag my fingers across his ribs, smiling as his muscles twitch. I feel his lips curl where they're still pressed against mine, and I know the memory he's recalling. I was relentless the day I discovered he was ticklish. The Archangel Michael, the mighty warrior, brought down low by my mortal fingers on his ribs.

I'd never heard him laugh like that before.

The click of his belt buckle being undone and the sound of his zipper being dragged down cuts through the quiet as I slide off Michael's lap. An instant later, he's on his knees on the ground before me and I hear the sound of ripping denim as he tears the offending button off the front of my pants, the time for restraint forgotten.

Michael looks almost feral as he kneels down before me. Firelight flickers across his bare chest, streaks of crimson and deep orange cutting through the shadows. His pants hang undone, his knees spread wide as he watches and waits. His eyes are wild and wanton, but still somehow reverent, as though I'm some long forgotten idol or goddess who demands her followers prostrate themselves in the dirt.

He crawls forward, closing the scant foot that separates us and draws his hands up the back of my thighs to cup my ass, his fingers hooking on the back of my ruined jeans and tugging them over my hips to catch at my knees. I wiggle against him, kicking off my boots, the heavy soles thudding loudly in the grass. The jeans follow a moment later, leaving me naked but for a tiny triangle of black fabric.

He nudges apart my legs, tracing a fingertip delicately over that thin layer of cotton still separating us, the touch so intimate, so worshipful that I hold my breath. He's on his knees between my thighs, and my breath hitches as I wait for him to rip through the fabric barrier and take me.

Instead, Michael backs off, lifting one of my legs up high enough to kiss the instep of my foot before moving upwards, his breath hot against the tense muscle of my calf. I can feel him almost purring, the low rumble in his chest a growl of possession that something deep within me remembers and aches for. He follows his path upward, the feather-light touches of his fingertips a sharp contrast to the rasp of the stubble darkening his jaw against my inner thigh. My fingers claw into the ground, my nails gouging into the dry earth beneath me.

The sound of more fabric tearing cuts through the night, and some tiny part of me is almost amused this sudden caveman bravado that has Michael shredding my clothes in my backyard, but a much larger part of me *understands*.

With that last impediment gone, Michael doesn't hesitate. He licks a wide line between my legs, the flat of his tongue tasting every part of me, and I'm thrown back to the villa and the sea air and a year's worth of days and nights tangled in each other.

How did we let this be taken from us?

Michael looks up at me, the firelight glinting in his eyes, and he nips my inner thigh, snapping me back to the here and now, and I need to touch him. I cup the back of his head, my fingers searching for purchase in that close-cropped hair, and I hold his blazing stare for as long as I can.

It isn't long.

My eyes fall shut as my vision whites out, my thighs shaking under Michael's touch. It hits me hard and fast, pleasure spiraling out from my fingertips down to my toes, heat lightning pulsing through my veins.

It's only when my breathing finally starts to even out and I open my eyes again that Michael lifts his head, his burning gaze still focused on me. He kisses his way up my body, pressing his lips to my hipbones and along each rib, letting his hands roam freely across whatever skin his mouth misses.

The fire pulsates and throbs, the flames moving like a living creature in the worn fire pit, and Michael's mouth is on mine. My lips part for him without hesitation, and I taste myself on his tongue. The rough denim of his jeans rubs against my thighs, and this time I'm the one clawing at fabric with desperation, pushing his open jeans down his thighs.

Michael's breath stutters when I wrap my hand around his cock and he thrusts into my hand.

"Michael," I whisper, and I don't recognize my own voice. I sound broken, vocal cords blown out with need, and I know this is a mistake, but regrets are for tomorrow.

All that matters now is skin on skin, flesh on flesh as the fire burns in the small hours of the morning when even New Orleans slumbers. We're both scorching, and I'm going to lose my mind if he isn't inside me soon.

I tilt my hips forward, that frantic movement telling Michael *yes* and *please* and *now* far more effectively than any words. For once, he takes the hint and he rolls his hips, the muscles of his back flexing as he pushes into me.

I dig my fingers into his shoulder blades, my brain idly imagining his wings are pulsing in time with the rocking of his hips. . . deeper and deeper until he bottoms out. The ground beneath me is hard, his jeans are rough against my over-sensitized skin, and I'm fairly sure there's a rock jabbing into my lower back but nothing matters beyond Michael's breath as he pants raggedly into my neck. It's almost too much, this sensory overload, and it takes everything I have to not simply screw my eyes shut and ride the waves of pleasure.

But I don't. I keep my eyes open even as I cling to him. Michael hauls me upward and off the ground, sitting back on his heels until we're face to face with the flickering fire lighting both our faces. Nose to nose, and there's nowhere to hide for either of us.

Not anymore.

"Elissa–" I cut Michael off with a kiss as our bodies move together, blocking him from saying whatever declaration brewing in his mind.

Let me have this. Don't promise me more when we both know what you'll choose in the end. Just let me have this night.

I break the kiss abruptly, biting back a wail as I come, inner muscles clenching and fluttering around Michael's length, and he follows a moment later, any threads of restraint having long since snapped. Michael shudders in my arms as he spills inside me, his face buried in the sweaty tangle of my hair.

The fire stutters before going out, plunging us into darkness as we hover on the border of nighttime and dawn. The first streaks of grey haven't begun lightening the horizon just yet, and that's enough for me. Michael and I stand up on unsteady legs, and I lead him into the house.

I should be doing anything but leading him into my bedroom, but that doesn't stop me from yanking the curtains closed to block out the coming dawn for a bit longer. I have grass in my hair and dirt on my knees. I want a shower and a long stretch of uninterrupted sleep, but I forget all about that when Michael kicks off his jeans and climbs into my bed.

I hesitate just for a moment, the scuffed wood floors cool under my bare feet, before crawling in beside him.

Just let me have this night.

I WAKE up to bright sunlight peeking around the edges of the curtains and the warm length of Michael's body pressed against my back. One muscular arm is slung over my waist and his breath puffs against the back of my neck.

It would be so easy to burrow into his arms and let my eyes slip closed. To let the past be the past. To forgive.

But he's given me no reason to believe that he won't snap to attention when Heaven calls again. After so much time I can't pretend to know him anymore.

I slither out of bed slowly to delay the inevitable confrontation a few more hours. The fact that he's sleeping as deeply as he is reminds me that he's not at full strength yet. Angels don't need to sleep at all. Caila sleeps like a cat with the slightest noise waking her, dozing more out of boredom than actual need for rest. If I managed to wriggle out of his arms without waking him up, he's still healing.

I pad across the room and grab the first things my fingers touch in my closet, glad that the utilitarian style of my clothing makes dressing easy. Black always goes with black. My boots are still somewhere in the back yard and I creep out of the room, my bare feet silent on the cool floors.

I pause in the doorway, feeling the pull between us that always drew us back to each other.

I still love him. Some part of me never stopped. Years of

anger and hurt never managed to erase it, and last night only reminded me of that even more.

I still love him, but I can't go through this again.

Resting on the kitchen counter is a torn piece of paper with an address written in a neat, feminine hand. Grace, of course.

I glance back at the darkened hallway once more before grabbing my helmet off the floor and climbing into the stolen car to pick up my bike on the way.

Time to plan.

California
1963

Palm trees and sunshine. Big cars and gleaming white smiles that hide a generation scarred by war and loss and right at the center of it is Caila.

Her pale blonde hair is set in an immaculate halo of pin curls, and a buttercup yellow sheath dress clings to her hips. Dainty white heels click on the tile floor as she paces, her curls flouncing just a bit with each step as she casts worried glances to the two young women sitting in the opulence of the lobby of the Casa Del Mar.

I've had little reason to change my opinion of angels in the last millennia. The few I've encountered over the years still treat humans as little more than animals to be controlled or commodified. Beyond those chance encounters, I've done my best to give any celestials a wide berth.

And yet, here is this anxious blonde angel dressed like a cupcake begging me for aid. I can't help being curious.

I ignore the look of disdain the concierge shoots my way as I pass through the gleaming double doors into the lobby.

I'm well aware of how wildly out of place I look with my black cigarette pants and straight hair in this palace of pastels and pin curls, but after centuries of enduring corsets and hoop skirts and yards upon yards of unwieldy fabric for the sake of appearances, I've embraced the Beatnik look wholeheartedly.

If the angel has any opinions on my sartorial choices, she keeps them to herself. Her scarlet lips split into a relieved smile and she rushes forward, taking both of my hands in hers and squeezing them like we're lifelong friends.

"You came!" she exclaims. "I didn't think you would, and I didn't know what else to do to help them." Her words tumble over themselves as she rushes to speak as though she expects me to turn on my heel and walk out.

Angel or not, it's hard to dislike her.

"I've heard about you. About the things you do for women. How you help them when they have nowhere else to turn." Caila looks over my shoulder to the two women, relaxing slightly when she confirms no one has snatched them away in the last sixty seconds. "The blonde one. She's important." Caila blinks, and I'm shocked at how upset she looks for a moment before she schools her face back into angelic placidity. "I've been trying to protect her bloodline for so long, and I always fail. Her friend, the child. . . they're innocent and they should be shielded from evil as well, but *she* is important."

I turn around to see the smaller of the two women sit down next to her friend. Her hair is twisted into a messy attempt at the flawlessly teased and set style Caila wears, but a few curls escape the cage of pins and hairspray to tumble down her neck. Her hand rests on her crying friend's shoulder reassuringly before fishing through her purse to bring out a handkerchief. Her friend dabs at her swollen eyes, leaving black mascara smears on the delicate white fabric.

"They're all important," I murmur before turning back to Caila. "Introduce me then."

Caila leads me across the lobby, fixing the glowering concierge with a sweetly mollifying smile before stopping in front of the overstuffed sofa the women are perched on. "Ladies," she says pointedly, "this is Elissa."

The blonde squeezes her friend's arm before standing up and extending her hand. "Serafine Celestin." She glances back at her friend. "This is Milly. She's in between last names."

The three of us unconsciously seem to bracket Milly where she sits, still delicately rubbing her eyes with the handkerchief. A deep purple bruise colors her cheekbone, half-hidden under thick makeup that her tears have started to wash away. She shifts and the powder blue coat enveloping her falls open, revealing her heavily pregnant stomach straining the front of her dress. She has to be close to term.

That explains the sudden urgency then.

Milly struggles to her feet, her round belly throwing off her balance, but she shrugs off Serafine's helping hand. Terrified and battered she may be, but Milly isn't broken, and she isn't about to sit quietly while we figure out her future.

"We're from New Orleans," she says, a thick drawl coloring her voice that calls up white gloves, magnolia blossoms, and southern propriety. "I married John when we were too young. I'm not going to say that he changed. This was always in him, but once I was his property he didn't care about hiding it anymore." She pulls the coat a bit tighter around herself despite the warmth of the room, her eyes darting to the steady stream of businessmen and pampered wives passing through the lobby as though she expects her husband to be hidden among them.

"He followed us here," she adds. "As soon as I found out I was pregnant, I knew I had to run before he killed us both, so I got on a Greyhound and came out to meet my best friend."

She reaches across the space between them and squeezes Serafine's hand.

Serafine smiles brightly, but it doesn't reach her eyes. "That's right," she says, and I hear a flinty resolve in her voice that makes me begin to understand why Caila is so insistent that this one is special. "We're going to live on the beach and get suntans. Maybe one day we'll even get a convertible. I'm sure we can find one where we can fit a baby seat."

Milly laughs, brittle and sad under the thinnest veneer of hope, and I can't ignore the two of them anymore than I could leave Tanith starving in the streets or Melita to die in the brothel. I catch Caila's eye and nod.

Caila wraps one arm around Milly and leads her toward the hotel bar. "Let's see if we can't get you a glass of water," she coos, leaving me alone with Serafine.

"Comfort and prayers are all well and good, but they won't fix this." Serafine drops down onto an empty leather armchair, the mask of optimism disappearing once her friend is out of sight. "I don't have much trust in her kind. I've never had a reason to, but Caila means well." She seems to have almost forgotten I'm here until she looks up, focusing that steel-grey gaze on me with laser intensity.

"I've heard about you. I'm looking for a solution that's a bit more permanent." This woman, barely more than a girl, is sitting in a hotel lobby calmly asking me to murder her friend's husband, and I know I'll be grilling Caila soon enough to find out what interest Heaven has in Serafine Celestin.

"He won't stop. And now that he knows about the baby, he's got the law on his side," she scoffs. "Man's law, after all. Caila thinks everyone can be redeemed, but I think you and I know differently."

I don't need the angelic ability to read people to see the scars Heaven has left across Serafine. Even now, she watches them both where they sit at the hotel bar as though she doesn't quite trust Caila enough to let her out of her sight.

"Her parents, they're good people, but they're not rich." She opens up the slim white leather pocketbook tucked under her arm and pulls out a smooth lacquered cigarette case. She lights one with a hand that trembles ever so slightly, taking a deep drag before she continues. "John's Daddy has half the police force in in New Orleans in his pocket. I tried for so long to get her to leave him, but the bastard swore he'd ruin her father's business if she ever tried."

After that initial drag Serafine ignores the cigarette until it's one long cylinder of ash balanced precariously between her long fingers. She glances at it and wrinkles her nose briefly before flicking it into the crystal ashtray on the side table. "Her parents spent their whole life building that bakery, and John was more than vindictive enough to destroy it."

I listen silently. Serafine has been the strong one for them both. The protector. A guard dog in a pretty dress. No one would ever see her coming.

"She never even telephoned me. I answered the doorbell one day six months ago, and there she was with red eyes and a suitcase," A tiny smile crosses her lips at the memory. "I miss New Orleans, but I had to leave too." Before I can form the words to ask why, she shakes her head. "I know the only reason Caila is really here is because of me, but none of this is about me. "

Her fingers idly toy with a delicate gold locket resting against her collarbone. The metal is old, specks of tarnish clinging to the surface and I wonder whose picture rests inside. "Not this time."

HE ISN'T difficult to find.

After stowing Milly in a room at the hotel with Serafine keeping a watchful eye on her, I go hunting. Caila trails me like a conscience, and I know long before I pound on the white-lacquered door of his room at the Hollywood Roosevelt that she won't make this easy.

When John answers it's easy to see why Milly was taken in by him. He has the kind of boyish good looks that make juries forgive and police officers say "she must have been asking for it." An impeccably cut cream suit hugs his slim form, and a glass of no doubt expensive scotch dangles carelessly in his hand. He barely gives me a glance, but when his eyes rest on Caila he's suddenly all smiles.

"I think you ladies might be in the wrong room, but who would I be to question such a fortuitous mistake?" he drawls. He flings open the door and ushers us both inside. Caila's so taken aback that I swear she forgets she's an angel for a moment, looking every bit the flustered southern belle she's pretending to be.

"Your wife sent us," I say, my voice cutting through his flirtation, and the change is instantaneous. His face darkens, that innocent schoolboy smirk twisting into something ugly and malicious. He swings his head to glare at me, and I meet his stare without flinching. That incenses him even more.

"I'm not surprised to see that trashy little bitch fell in with someone like you," he sneers, his momentary infatuation with Caila apparently forgotten. "I don't care if she lives or dies, but that child in her is mine."

Caila snaps out of her stupor and lays a restraining hand on John's arm, and he shoves her back.

Or he tries.

Caila draws her power around her and the tawny gold of her wings fills the room. She's no longer a bubbly creature dressed in pastels and lace, smiling sweetly at all who look upon her. From one moment to the next, the strength of

Heaven swirls around her, and for the first time the smarmy confidence dripping from Milly's husband falters.

"You have been judged, John Desbois." The color drains from his face leaving a sickly grey pallor that a nice haircut and expensive suit can't hide. "Do you repent for your crimes and your cruelties?" Caila demands, spreading her wings wide until the room seems to be filled with nothing but golden feathers and righteous feminine anger.

"Y-yes," John stammers. "Of course." He agrees far too quickly, dropping to his knees without hesitation as he reaches one grasping hand out to touch Caila's wingtips. I hover at the edge of the scene, wondering how she can restrain herself from recoiling from his touch. "I didn't believe before," he says, his eyes wide as saucers as he stares at her wings. "I'll go to church. I'll be a good husband."

Caila drops to her knees beside him, and she really believes him. My presence is forgotten again, and I'm still far too shocked that a being that has lived for thousands of years can still be so naïve.

"There's no need to kneel before me," she murmurs, resting one delicate hand on his head, offering her blessing before leaning closer and whispering, "Heaven forgives you."

Heaven might forgive him, but I don't.

It's all far too easy. John is a picture of contrition before Caila, dragging up fragments of prayers likely pushed into his head by a well-meaning parish priest, swearing that he'll dedicate his life to bringing others into the light.

I slip out the door. The thick pile of the deep green carpet looks like moss crushed under the toe of my boot, and the bright floral of the wallpaper lining the hallway catches the light of the heavy crystal chandelier dangling from the ceiling. In her sunshine yellow dress, Caila looks like she belongs in this Eden of wallpaper and carpeting while I look like a streak of blight killing the flowers.

I lean against the wall, my eyes slipping shut as I wait for Caila, wondering where this sudden maudlin streak came from.

Angels. I should have known better than to get involved with another angel, however well-meaning she might be.

The low murmurs of their voices filter through the crack in the door, a slow drone that can only be a prayer, and I wonder if Milly's prayers would have been answered if her best friend had been someone unimportant.

When Caila emerges from the room a few minutes later there's no trace of smugness in her. Her entire face is radiant with such genuine joy that she helped heal this broken soul that it makes me want to believe.

But I've seen too much, and this was far too easy.

JOHN IS SMARTER than any of us gave him credit for.

Days pass without incident. Caila, Milly, and even wary Serafine begin to relax. After the third day slips past without any fists on the door, the creeping dread starts to uncoil from my stomach, and even I wonder if maybe, just maybe, I might have been wrong.

I hoped I was wrong.

As Milly naps, Serafine and Caila tell me of just why Heaven is so interested in the life of this petite blonde, unwinding a story of holy bloodlines and murderous angels. Serafine speaks in reverent tones of her mother Rose, lovely and lost behind the walls of an asylum.

Milly wasn't the first to flee the Crescent City for a new beginning with palm trees and ocean breezes.

"What about your father?" I ask. Some part of me knows what her answer will be before I form the words, like recognizing like and the easy way she spoke of permanence in dealing with John.

"The fire marshal said it was a gas leak," Serafine says, glancing over from where she stands on the terrace, staring out at the cloudless sky. She clicks open the polished brass of her lighter, touching the tiny orange flame to the pristine white tip of another cigarette that she'll take one drag of before letting it burn down to the filter. "Those old houses, you know. The whole place went up." She turns back to stare out at the ocean, her thumb still rubbing the warm metal of the lighter.

"He didn't make it out."

Like recognizes like.

The soft breeze ruffles Serafine's hair, and I remember seeing the broken form of my father tossed into the gutter outside the tavern, the stench of cheap wine and decaying shellfish still soaked into his skin. I followed him home that night, tracked his weaving steps back to the cramped dwelling that I once called home. His unsteady steps lead him down to the water, to the uneven paths and slippery rocks.

And he slipped. The water closed over his head, drink and age and human weakness turning his arms to lead. I knew I could dive in and drag him to the shore and pound his back to force the brackish water from his lungs.

The daughter he reviled saving his wretched life. It almost had a poetry to it, but it was drowned out by the memory of that bag of coins jingling in his hands as he sold me off to the first bidder.

I walked away when no more bubbles came to the surface.

THREE DAYS in even the most decadent hotel suite has us all going stir crazy, and Milly is begging to go back to the apartment and sleep in her own bed. Fully assured that her divine intervention was successful, Caila's all too eager to agree. I'm still not so sure, but spending so much time in such close proximity to an angel still makes me twitchy, and I tell myself that I'm eager to get back to my life. . . whatever that was.

I can't bring myself to go far.

Seven days have passed since I watched John drop to his knees with repentance on his lips, and still I stay close, hidden out of sight as I watch them both fall back into the routines of their small, mortal lives.

The apartment Serafine and Milly share is small and decorated in swaths of bright colors. It's a cheerful space with big windows and a scrawny lemon tree growing in a pot by the front door. The next time I see it, the doorknob is caved in, and I hesitate for the smallest instant before pushing it open, knowing what I'm going to see.

Serafine is sprawled face down on the floor, just inside the door. I drop down beside her and press my fingers against her throat. Her pulse pounds strong and steady. She's out cold but very much alive.

But Milly.

The smell hits me first, that thick copper tang that catches in the back of your throat, and I see Milly flat on her back. Her dark hair hides the blood at first until the thick red liquid spreads even further, soaking into the mint green carpeting.

I prod the wound ever so gently, moving aside the matted strands to assess the damage, praying to a God I never trusted that it's just scalp blood vessels making it look much worse than it is.

I see cracked bone, and I know.

The ambulance is a daze of flashing lights and brisk, loud voices. They shove me in a corner as they force oxygen into Milly's unresponsive lungs. Serafine fights the medic trying to examine her, sobbing Milly's name over and over again. We pull up to the hospital, sterile and bright and so very helpless.

I'm left in the waiting room, surrounded by broken limbs

and car accidents, falls and stabbings, endless reminders of the fragility of the mortal body.

Caila appears an hour later. Red stains on the hem of the pale pink dress she wears, pastel linen streaked with gore, and I can almost see her kneeling down to touch the bloody carpet, using her angelic senses to read whatever echoes of Milly still cling to the fibers.

She sits next to me on the stiff backed waiting room chairs, and when she speaks her voice is flat and dull, the animation gone from her.

"She just wanted him to leave. He showed up at her door, raving about how God had chosen him for greatness, and now she had to come home with him." Caila clasps her hands together and I can see the drying blood in the creases of her fingers. "I just made it worse."

"Milly's dead."

We both snap out of it to look up and see Serafine standing in front of us, a vivid bruise blooming across her temple, and a paper bag rattling with a prescription bottle in her hand. Her face is a mask.

"The baby made it. It's a boy." Serafine's voice wavers for just a moment before she yanks herself back in control, and I almost pity the angel that tries to attack her one day. "He cannot have that baby."

I look up at Serafine and nod, searching her eyes for the anger I deserve, the blame. It's not there. This one is used to failures and betrayals, and I won't be the cause of another. "I'm going to kill him," I say.

It's Caila that breaks the silence with one word as we both get to our feet and follow Serafine through the double doors.

"Good."

10
MICHAEL

I wake up to an empty bed, and no part of me is surprised.

I feel wrung out. Between the toxic magic that tore through my system, dredging up long buried memories and the dream-like encounter with Elissa, I still don't feel like myself.

I wonder who that even is anymore.

I can still feel her on my skin. Her scent surrounds me in this tangle of plain white sheets, and it's so tempting to stay. To hope for just a bit longer that last night was a new beginning and not the ending we were both denied for so long, but Caila is still missing.

As Elissa said, it's not about me.

The house is worlds away from the villa by the cliffs, and I quickly realize that every personal touch in this small structure is from Caila's hands. I duck into Caila's bedroom to retrieve my shirt from floor, grimacing at the stiff patch of dried blood decorating the front, and I can't help pausing at the difference in the spaces.

This room is a museum or a temple to the strange and

beautiful objects humanity creates for their own amusement. Each item in Caila's space is perfectly curated from the artfully weathered wood of the platform bed and the tangle of pale pink blankets to the trinkets and books lined up on the gold and glass of the side table. Yet for an angel, it's all unneeded. Nothing but noise and distraction from our duties.

Even those of my brothers and sisters who spend years or even decades stationed on Earth rarely live like this. I spent a year with Elissa in Sidon, and though I left my mark on her life and her soul, there was nothing to leave behind in the house.

A chunk of hematite carved into the crude shape of a bird sits on the windowsill, the light bouncing off it making the stone look like quicksilver. I pick it up, turning the warm stone over in my hands and wondering what about this tiny thing entranced her so. Angels have no use for *things*, but I'm beginning to wonder if this was yet another lie I told myself.

Caila surrounds herself with things. The living room is still a wreck. The damaged furniture has been flipped upright and the shattered crockery swept away, but Elissa left the rest to be dealt with later. And while I don't pretend to know Elissa's tastes anymore, I can't picture her concerning herself with selecting coordinating armchairs and porcelain teacups.

A thick book rests on the cracked and charred surface of a desk, the leather cover worn soft by years of handling. I flip it open and see the Enochian text filling up the page. I expect spells or even angelic lore, but instead I find a diary. The first entry is dated 1963, and my name on the page catches my eye.

My garrison would say I care too much for these humans. Perhaps they're right. But each time I return home I see nothing but Uriel descending deeper into madness and rage. As he hides in the garden, Raphael spends his days studying lore and prophecies so much that he fails to see the world outside his cloister. And Gabriel hasn't been seen for years.

Then there is Michael. I don't speak his name to Elissa. This tentative partnership we've created in the aftermath of California isn't yet strong enough to bear such scrutiny. I wonder if she thinks I'm unaware of her history with Heaven.

In Heaven, Michael is like a ghost of his former self. He follows orders without question, accepting mission after mission and the trail of blood and bodies behind him grows.

I cannot be the only one who remembers the days when the world was young and the archangels were whole – when Lucifer lit the stars and Uriel coaxed the first seeds to life. When Michael was not a broken solider with dead eyes.

I slam the book shut.

I never noticed her. One more angel in the crowd of thousands. I vaguely recall pale hair and a wistful smile, but beyond that nothing. Yet somehow she saw it all and has been by Elissa's side for sixty years.

I almost open the book up again. Hundreds of pages filled with her tiny hand. Her history. Elissa's history. I want to know it all, but I want to hear it from her lips and not cold paper and ink.

I stalk away from the book's temptation and back down the narrow hallway. I pause in the doorway to Elissa's Spartan quarters. Only the trunk and a single painting give any hints of the occupant's personality.

I'm not foolish enough to touch the trunk. Elissa had a similar one back in Sidon that held her most powerful tools. The surface of the wood nearly shimmers with magic, the wards wrapped around it as thick as those surrounding the mansion.

The painting beckons me closer. The large canvas is covered in swirls of black and the deepest blues and greens. A storm nearly boils the ocean, and the waves caught on the canvas are the type to dash a ship's hull upon the rocks and pull sailors to their deaths. It's nature's violence barely contained within a frame, and I can almost hear the sea crashing against the cliffs as the thunder rumbles around me.

A few of the clouds near the edge of the canvas are lighter, as though the sun is fighting to cut through the screen of black clouds. No beacon of hope splits the sky though, no bright ray of sunshine to promise the storm has passed. The sea is still in control.

The sea always wins.

I shake my head at the thought and force myself to walk away, out the back door and into the bright midday sun. Elissa's boots are missing from the yard, but I see the ruined black scraps of her clothes in a messy pile beside the charred metal of the firepit.

In the harsh light of day it's just a patch of overgrown grass hemmed in by a sagging chain-link fence, but last night. . . last night it felt like we were at the edge of the world again. Alone but for the wind and the fire and each other.

I walked away once. I let myself be called to heel and I smiled obediently as Metatron and Heaven and Father tightened the leash. Thousands of years, and what have I done but bring more death to this world? Many that I killed deserved death, but did they all?

Was Lucifer truly so wrong to question? He called me God's most favored son. We Archangels have always been the most favored in Heaven's eyes and yet one of us is Fallen, another lost to madness and death, one lives in books and scrolls, and one hides from us all.

And then there is me.

God's Cudgel.

God's Blade.

God's Mortar Shell.

If this is what it means to be the favored son, I don't want it anymore. I'm not sure if I ever did.

I spread my wings, already seeing that poisonous mansion

in my eyes and ready to tear down the walls to prove myself to her.

"Are you stupid or just suicidal?"

The bored drawl of my brother's voice stops me. I turn back to the house to see Lucifer standing on the porch, looking immaculate as always in his black suit. He descends the stairs slowly, perfectly looking the part of petulant younger brother.

"Neither," I reply curtly.

Lucifer scoffs. "You're headed back to the place where you nearly died twelve hours ago. The Michael I knew was a better strategist than that so that just leaves death wish." Lucifer thrusts a black button-down shirt into my hands, giving the ruined tee I'm wearing a disdainful look. "Even in New Orleans you can't exactly walk around the city with a stab wound through your shirt without raising a few eyebrows."

Rolling my eyes, I yank off the shirt and drop it on the ground next to the torn remnants of Elissa's clothes. The shirt Lucifer brought is snug across my shoulders, no doubt one of his, but it'll do.

Lucifer is staring down at the pile of ripped black cloth by my feet. A wry smile curls across his lips as he realizes just what they are, and I prepare myself for the inevitable onslaught of snide comments. "Did you just come here to give me a shirt and mock me?" I ask.

The smile on Lucifer's face melts away, and his face is serious when he speaks. "I always had a soft spot for her. She reminds me of myself." Lucifer lets that comment hang in the air for far longer than is comfortable for either of us before pushing on. "How do you think she stayed out of the Pit for all these years? I couldn't take a truly good soul even if I wanted to, remember? And under all that anger and all that blood, hers is still pure."

The sun beats down on both of us, the sky bleached white from the unrelenting rays, but Lucifer doesn't blink as he takes another step closer to me, trying to goad me into backing up. "You don't deserve her. You never did."

Hot jealousy uncoils in my stomach like a poisonous creature. I've always known it was Lucifer who gave Elissa the double-edged gift of immortality, but I never allowed myself to consider just what she traded for it. Was she just his protégé? Yet another tool for Lucifer's vengeance on Heaven and most of all me?

Or had she ever been something more?

"What is she to you?" I hiss.

Lucifer's brow furrows for just an instant before fading into a look of astonishment. "Are you serious?" he demands. A look of hurt flickers across his face for an instant before sliding into familiar anger. "Betrayal was your domain, Michael. Not mine. And certainly not hers." Lucifer takes a step back, but keeps his black gaze fixed on me, making sure I'm well aware that this isn't a retreat. "If I had found my way inside your great love's robes all those years ago do you honestly think I would have waited until now to throw it in your face?"

I can't disagree with that fact.

Lucifer doesn't pause in his diatribe. "You chose our Father and two thousand more years of Heavenly bullshit, and for what? You can't tell me you enjoy being God's chosen pitbull anymore, if you ever did in the first place." When I don't interrupt, Lucifer trails off. The neighborhood symphony of blaring car horns and muffled bass from a rattling car stereo a few houses down cuts through the silence, but Lucifer is as unrelenting in his search for answers as he ever was in Heaven.

His voice is low when he speaks again, the perpetual anger that suffuses him draining away into a look of resigned weariness that could be my own. "Tell me the truth, Michael."

I could lie. Once I was good at it, at least at lying to myself. Lucifer would see through the deception as he always did, but maybe for once he'd let it go.

Not likely.

"I envied you."

Lucifer chuckles, the familiar mockery rising to the surface again. "You do remember I was in Hell?"

I smile sadly at that. As if I could forget. "You weren't just a good soldier. You questioned. You made your own choices."

"And you saw how well that worked out for me until recently," Lucifer replies before adding, "Grace would say we're having a moment."

"I can knock another house on you if it helps."

Lucifer lets out a bark of laughter, and it's so genuine that I'm taken aback at the sudden flood of memories of who we both were long before the Fall. Some tiny part of me dares to hope that maybe I can recapture some semblance of that again.

"Where is she?" I ask, finally relenting.

"Where do you think?" Lucifer answers. "She showed up at our door this morning with grass in her hair and immediately started plotting with Grace. I'm guessing the arrow was the least eventful portion of your night."

I can't help glowering at him and Lucifer rolls his eyes. "I'm the one who spent eons locked in Hell, Michael, but most days you seem more maudlin than I do."

"Last night doesn't matter." I want to believe in second chances, that something more than random fate crossed our paths again after all these years, but I still have far too many doubts. "She still hates me. She should hate me."

Lucifer stands still in the middle of the yard, the amused banter quickly giving way to irritation. "I'm going to say this once, brother, and once only," he snaps. "Make a fucking decision." I bristle at his insinuation, opening my mouth to interject an argument, but Lucifer's patience has run out.

"You made the wrong choice all those years ago. You've regretted it ever since, and it's taken you this long to admit it." Lucifer paces, the dying grass crunching under his feet as the frenetic energy that always seems to follow him boils over. "You convinced yourself what you did was right and proper and for her own good, but all those lies you told yourself have finally come crashing down, and you have to face the cold hard reality of truth." Lucifer's eyes narrow as he finally pauses, and I want to put my fist in his face, tentative fraternal affection be damned.

"You did all this for what?" he spits. "Father? We don't matter to him anymore than they do. He's gone somewhere and found himself a new toy, and the humans are left in the dust just as we were. You threw away your one chance at happiness for that?"

I round on Lucifer, wildly telegraphing my punch. Lucifer dodges easily, but doesn't bother throwing one of his own. Instead he rocks back on his heels, just out of arm's reach and waits in infuriating silence.

I want to yell, want to scream in my true voice until I splinter all the glass in the city and the car alarms drown out Lucifer's words.

But I don't. My voice is barely above a whisper when I speak, finally giving voice to the decision that I've let haunt me for centuries.

"You think it was easy?" Something in Lucifer's face changes, some flicker of understanding, and it gives me the strength to continue. "I did it to save her. I didn't choose Heaven. I chose to keep her alive." The words fall out of me like the purging of sickness, and I sit down in the grass, the weight of admitting the truth after so long pressing me into the earth.

Humans say they feel lighter after confession, as though their burdens have been eased. All I feel is the weight of every last year spent without her.

The bright sun burning through my closed eyelids darkens, and I feel Lucifer's hand on my shoulder. I peel open my eyes to look up at him.

Once, years beyond telling ago, we were closer than twins. When the world was young I watched my brother light the stars, watched his joy at bringing light into the darkness. He was my confidant and my closest friend until humanity and pride became the wedge that drove us apart.

Pride. It was always seen as Lucifer's sin, but I'm just as guilty.

The Lucifer staring down at me isn't the angry, vengeful creature I remember clashing with over the years or even the wary ally of the last few weeks. Looking down at me with dawning comprehension of just what I did is the Lightbringer, the brother I thought lost to the darkness forever.

For the first time I can look at him without hearing the crack of wing bones breaking.

"Metatron," he says.

I nod stiffly, and Lucifer takes my hand, pulling me none too gently to my feet. He is, after all, still Lucifer.

"You get something very few do, Michael. A second chance." Lucifer spreads his wings, and I follow suit. We've wasted too much time already. In the moment before we take to the skies, Lucifer pauses, fixing me with that black stare and pinning me to the spot. "But unless you truly want that chance and intend to follow through, don't even try. She won't give you a third."

Then we're airborne, and I'm following Lucifer, our wings cutting through the skies as he traces the path back to the home he shares with Grace. He tosses his last comment into the wind.

"And I'm fairly sure she still has that crossbow bolt."

LUCIFER EASES OPEN the front door with a casual familiarity, stepping over the ginger cat lounging on the welcome mat. The animal blinks at me, eyeing me for a moment with its bored green stare before stretching exaggeratedly and going back to sleep.

"Honey, I'm home!" Lucifer can't keep the amusement out of his voice, and I wonder what my chances are at ever regaining that easy intimacy with Elissa.

"Back here!" Grace's muffled voice comes from the other end of the hallway, and we walk through the narrow passage.

Elissa's voice filters back to me, sure and offering no space for argument. "It has to be me. We saw what that place did to Michael, and Fallen or not Lucifer is still an angel."

"I'm not an angel," Grace protests.

"And I'm not going to be the one who suggests to Lucifer that I take you in there."

The small space of Grace's kitchen comes into view, and both women are sitting at the table as they plan. Grace's back is to me, but there's no hiding the frustration in her voice. "Look Elissa, I'm in this now too. I'm not a child or a weak little human anymore. Are we all conveniently forgetting that I killed an archangel?"

Elissa notices the two of us skulking in the doorway. Her gaze slips coolly over me before she shoots Lucifer a look that says, *I tried.*

Her hair hangs in wet waves as though she just stepped out of the shower, and when I move into the room I smell the sweet scent of ripe pomegranate that emanates from the damp stands.

Grace cuts her eyes between the two of us, and there's no mistaking why Lucifer adores her. She may look like sweetness and light on the surface, but there's a streak of deviousness in her that my brother is no doubt encouraging.

"Do you like my new shampoo, Michael? I think it smells lovely on Elissa," she purrs, getting up from her seat to twine herself around my brother. Lucifer is nearly choking as he tries to hold back his laughter.

We have too much history to turn into blushing fools, stammering over our words at Grace's rightful insinuation. But I'm well aware of her tells enough to know that the slight flush coloring Elissa's cheeks isn't due to a hot shower or the humidity the ancient air conditioner struggles to overcome.

It only lasts a moment before she shutters the heat simmering between us with the ruthless efficiency of slamming a lid over a boiling pot. She's all business when she pushes the piece of paper she and Grace were huddled over towards me. "Grace is right," she says, taking extra care to keep her fingers from brushing mine. "She and I have a shot at getting past the wards and disabling them from the inside. You and Lucifer won't make it through the gate until we do."

Scribbled across the paper are hasty drawings of dozens of wards, every sigil a mystical Keep Out sign screaming from the page. Without the magic infusing them they're harmless, but there's no mistaking that this is very bad. Last night was such a blur that I never got a decent look at them, but seeing every symbol sketched out in black and white proves that we certainly aren't dealing with an amateur that made one lucky shot.

"I'm sure that isn't all of them, but I took a closer look when I picked up my bike," she continues. One bare nail taps on the largest of the sigils, a circle cut through with a jagged line like a lightning bolt. "They're very angelically targeted. Whoever she is, she doesn't want Heaven seeing what she's up to or getting in." Her finger slides across the page to another drawing, this one made of several interlocking six-pointed stars. "Or getting out," she adds.

Lucifer's eyes haven't left Grace, and I wait for the inevitable ultimatum when he forbids her from taking part in this plan. It never comes. Instead, he steers her into the shadows of the hall, far enough away from us both to give the illusion of privacy.

His voice is a low murmur, but it's still impossible to miss. "I'm not going to try to stop you from going." The plea to be careful hangs unspoken, unneeded. I glance out of the corner of my eye to where they stand and see Lucifer twisting one of her blonde curls around his finger, a gesture I've seen him replay a hundred times. "Even if I tried, you'd just knock the door down anyway," he remarks.

Grace giggles at the private joke before pulling Lucifer back into the planning session.

My mind wanders as Elissa rattles off a list of increasing obscure ingredients she needs, scrawling them on the back of the paper strewn with the sigils.

Equals. Every expectation I've had about my brother has been flipped on its head. Lucifer is still impulsive and arrogant. He still indulges himself in whatever vice suits his fancy with little regard for the rules of Heaven or man, but somehow she has tempered that scorching anger that boiled down into cold hatred over the years into something new.

If the devil himself deserves a second chance, maybe I do as well.

Grace plucks the page from her hand and stares at the list. "Do you have this stuff? Because I'm guessing we won't find-" she squints at the word "-asphodel petals at the local Whole Foods."

Elissa shakes her head, the movement tousling her hair just enough that I can smell pomegranates again. "I have a few of the ingredients, but not close to everything we need. Caila and I haven't been back long enough to get all our contacts in order, but this city has a hundred botanicas and we don't have the time to waste sifting through the fake ones."

"Erzulie's as real as it gets," Grace interjects.

"Erzulie's still kicking around here fleecing tourists then?" Elissa asks. "Good for her. I can't see her going anywhere else." Elissa's on her feet and heading towards the front door an instant later.

Lucifer makes a move to follow her, but Grace stops him with a pointed look. The King of Hell rolls his eyes before affectionately muttering, "You're not subtle, you know."

I emerge into the bright sunlight to find Elissa leaning against Grace's car, her head tilted upward to face the sky. Her eyes are closed, and she doesn't open them when she speaks. "Grace is a meddler."

"She means well."

Elissa takes a deep breath before turning to me. She looks over my shoulder at the gaping front door, down at the ginger cat winding its slender body around my feet, at the car that roars a bit too fast down the residential street.

Anywhere but at me.

"I can't do this again, Michael." Her voice is barely above a whisper, and that hesitation is so unfamiliar, so wrong on her I want to destroy whatever caused it.

It's becoming easier and easier to understand Lucifer's hatred for Heaven.

I take a step closer, and her eyes flicker upward, finally meeting mine. The hot metal of the car presses against her back, and she's so close that the scent of pomegranates wafts around us, bringing me back to lazy days in her bed, Elissa's tongue curling around my fingertips as I press the ruby seeds to her lips.

I crush my lips to hers, and she tastes of black coffee instead of honey sweet fruit or bitter wine. Her hands stay pressed against the side of the car for too many seconds, and I nearly pull away until I feel her lips part beneath mine. My hands are in her hair, and her arms curl around my neck, dragging me down to meet her. I'm dimly aware of the creaking of Grace's feet on the front step and her hasty retreat back into the house, but then Elissa arches up against me and it all falls away.

There is no campfire, no flickering shadows to hide behind, and we are both as whole as we ever are. We don't have the excuse of a brush with death to explain away this sudden desperation for touch and taste. In the blazing sunlight on a sidewalk in New Orleans there is nothing to hide behind anymore.

I break the kiss first, pulling back the barest inch. Her breath is on my lips, and I want this to be a beginning, but I already feel her pulling away, shuttering herself against me.

I take a step back, giving her the space she's silently asking for.

She presses her lips together and takes a breath. This time she meets my eyes, and that icy blue stare tells me all I need.

"Tell Grace I know where that shop is. I'll meet you there."

I'm left standing on the sidewalk as she revs her bike engine and peels down the street alone.

11
ELISSA

Erzulie's shop hasn't changed in thirty years. There's a fresh coat of yellow paint on the door, the curls and slashes of her veve carved through layers of the golden lacquer, and the tourists posing outside are snapping photos with sleek cell phones instead of bulky Polaroids, but everything else is the same.

I push open the door to the dimly lit shop, and I almost expect them to look up – Serafine, her anger at the world finally tempered by love and happiness, however brief. Marianne couldn't have been more than fifteen when I knew them, all gangly limbs and messy hair and the wide uncomplicated smile that I'm sure Grace shared before Uriel ripped apart her world.

I blink and the memory fades like the faint curl of incense smoke wafting through the room.

"Elissa, it's been too long."

Erzulie is as unchanging as her shop. She walks around the counter, yards of ocean blue fabric swirling around her feet like a whirlpool, tiny braids wreathing her head like Medusa's serpents. She stands eye to eye with me, fixing me with that ageless scrutiny as she takes my hands in hers. "I'd heard you were back in town." At my raised eyebrow she adds, "You never manage to keep as low of a profile as you think you do."

The door bangs open as Lucifer saunters in, flipping the sign to closed as an afterthought. Michael follows at his heels, looking equal parts apologetic and uncomfortable. I'm not terribly surprised at his obvious discomfort. Caila was always a bundle of nervous energy anytime we ended up here. Angels tend to have a complex relationship with the old gods and spirits, and Erzulie is no exception.

She seems more amused than anything at Lucifer's posturing, and her face lights up when she sees Grace. "The Last still lives," she says, releasing my hands to clasp Grace's with almost maternal affection. "Prophecies always are tricky things." Her attention finally drifts to Michael, and even she looks surprised to see him inside her shop. "And the Archangel Michael. Whatever is the reason for this reunion of Heaven, Hell, and Earth? None of you tend to bother much with social calls."

It's Lucifer that speaks, his voice tight as he casts quick glances at Grace. I only have the vaguest details about Grace and Lucifer's interactions with Erzulie, but something happened in this shop that has Lucifer's hackles up, and it's not just celestial pretense.

"You seem to know everything that goes on in this city," he sneers. "And you've never crossed paths with an incredibly powerful witch who likes to kidnap angels?"

Erzulie's jaw tightens. She knows exactly who we're referring to, whether our target has ever darkened her doorstep or not. "I believe I know who you mean, though we're hardly on a first name basis." Lucifer scoffs, and Erzulie flashes him a sharp look before pressing on. "She and I run in very different circles. I don't traffic in the dead, and I don't corrupt."

"She's a necromancer," Lucifer finishes. "Lovely. We know what she wants Caila for then."

Grace takes a step toward me, and I know I must look stricken. The heavy iron chain from the vision flashes across my eyes.

Oh Caila. We're coming.

It's Erzulie that answers Grace's unspoken question. The rest of us already know. "If she has an angel, she's draining her like a battery. The dead can only provide so much. She can siphon power off their souls and make deals with demons, but that won't keep her from rotting from the inside out and she knows it. But an angel? That opens many new doors."

"Who the Hell is she?" I choke out.

Erzulie shakes her head. "I honestly don't know."

Lucifer snorts at that. "Another prophecy then? More cagey bullshit for us to wade through?"

Erzulie rounds on Lucifer as her already thin patience snaps. "I've seen those wards too, boy," she growls. "I know what they mean. You aren't the only one taking shots at Heaven, and I more than had my fill of it last time."

She glares at Michael, her expression stony. "Your kind tends to leave a mess that the rest of us are stuck cleaning up after."

An instant later, she's back to her usual inscrutable tranquility, calmly taking the list of ingredients from my numb hands and disappearing into the back room to fill them. I follow her through the doorway, the beaded curtain slipping over me like water.

"How much of this have you seen, Erzulie?" I demand, shoving aside the few strands of beads still caught on my shoulder, the stones clanking together like a necklace of bones. "How much of this do you know? I feel like we're all running blind but you've seen the full picture for decades!"

Erzulie ignores my outburst as she measures out dried

white petals, her quick fingers tying off the bag before moving onto another jar holding desiccated white bones. Her hands pause on the lid, and she takes a heavy breath.

"You think it's that simple?" she chides. Her voice is light, but when she turns to me there's only bleakness in her eyes. "Everything I see comes in pieces. You know as well as I do that following the breadcrumbs gets easier after centuries but you're still fumbling through the darkness." She looks over my shoulder at the curtain hiding us from the rest of the shop. "Do you think I wanted to send that girl to her death, or watch her mother pretend to be just another human, as though hiding would save them?"

"Erzulie," I begin only to trail off immediately. What could I say, after all? I'd watched Caila suffer at every loss, watched her bury the guilt and blame and sadness under a saccharine smile and a pastel dress. Finally I stammer, "It's not your fault," the words feeling as hollow now as they ever have.

"Of course it's not my fault," she agrees, twisting the lid and plucking two of the bleached white bones from the jar. "But it wasn't theirs either. And it's far from over."

The bronze bowl rests on the scarred lacquer of the desk, and I try to imagine Caila's horrified expression at my savagery of chopping ingredients on the bare wood. The conjured fire boils the viscous fluid, and Grace hovers at my elbow, leaning over my shoulder to stare at the tar-colored mixture.

"Magic isn't like baking a cake," I lecture, startling Grace just enough that she takes a quick step backward, giving me the room I need to work. "You don't just throw two cups of virgin's blood and a teaspoon of rosemary into a cauldron and become immortal."

I chop the asphodel roughly, the dried petals crumbling into pieces that smell of ashes and Hellfire. I scoop them into my palm and toss them all into the bowl. The mixture flares white for a moment before fading back into black.

"That being said," I continue, "Intent needs a guide sometimes. That's where this comes in."

Grace's curiosity gets the best of her again and she leans closer, inhaling the scent of freshly turned earth that emanates from the bowl. "Tell me again what this is going to do for us?" she asks.

"Not us. You and Lucifer." Grace's grey eyes widen at my admission but she doesn't balk. Serafine would be proud at her granddaughter's mettle. "Lucifer told me about the bond. I can work with that, but this isn't going to be easy for either of you."

Lucifer enters the room as if on cue, and if the situation wasn't so dire I'd be laughing at the image of the devil hovering in doorways and waiting his turn. Instead I take his hand in mine and hold it over the bowl. The steam rises around us as I press the hilt of a small dagger into Grace's palm, the Hell-forged metal blackened and scorched.

Grace only hesitates for a moment before drawing the tip of the blade across his palm. He rotates his hand so that the few bright drops of blood that well up drip into the bowl before the wound closes. When Lucifer's blood hits the surface the potion glows blindingly white and the sharp scent of ozone cuts through the air.

Grace hands the knife to Lucifer, and he takes her hand in his, tracing his thumb over her palm before making the cut. Grace doesn't wince at the sting, and Lucifer turns her hand so that gravity can do its work.

When Grace's blood hits the potion the fire immediately

goes out. The steam hangs in the air above the surface for a moment before clearing, revealing a liquid as clear as water.

"Did it work?" Grace asks tentatively.

"We'll know soon enough," I answer, grabbing the two shot glasses I'd found buried in the back of the cabinet and filling them with the concoction. "Bottoms up."

Lucifer smirks as he takes the glass, the sarcasm doing a poor job of hiding his apprehension. "Shot glasses?"

I shrug. "When in New Orleans."

They both knock back the potion without hesitating. Lucifer has never expressed much concern for his own safety so I'm not terribly surprised at his boldness, but Grace continues to impress me at every turn. No one who's ever met her could call her weak after this.

I watch them both, scrutinizing them for effects. Potions tend to be volatile, and one with this much power should work almost instantly. Lucifer's face is apprehensive as he focuses all his attention on Grace, worry furrowing his brow.

It hits Lucifer first, buckling his knees and driving him to the ground. Grace is by his side in an instant, lacing her fingers through his as he stares unseeingly up at her face.

I'd explained what would happen to them both on the street outside Erzulie's shop, that the potion would heighten the bond between them temporarily to let Grace tap into Lucifer's strength and invulnerability.

Considering what we're up against, the potion is a necessity, but like all magic it comes at a cost. A bridge like that isn't something I can just build without letting everything else through – thoughts, memories, sensations. It's all pouring through the bond both ways like a flash flood strong enough to bring the devil to his knees.

I only hope Grace is strong enough to come out from under the torrent of Lucifer's past unscathed.

Lucifer shrugs off the onslaught quickly enough, pushing

his own reactions aside out of concern for Grace. The look he gives her holds such bare emotion, protectiveness and respect and love overflowing in one expression that I turn away, feeling like an intruder.

Lucifer pushes himself upright, knife-edged tension rippling through him as he waits.

A few more seconds tick by before Grace inhales sharply, her fingers digging into Lucifer's shoulder as she wavers. Lucifer pulls her closer, lifting her onto the torn seat of the blue velvet couch, my presence entirely forgotten.

Grace's eyes are wild and unfocused, her senses lost inside the images flashing through her mind.

"I'm sorry," Lucifer breathes. "I'm so sorry."

Grace whimpers, the noise sounding confused but not painful, not yet. Lucifer cups her chin in his hand, trying to draw her focus to him. "Grace, Grace look at me. Stay with me." His voice is firm, his grip tight enough to force her out of the memory for an instant.

"Lu-Lucifer? It's all so bright–" her voice cuts off as she plunges back into the memory.

Lucifer looks up at me, his face a mask. "She's seeing the time before the Fall. It won't be bright for much longer."

Grace arches upward, an animal sob of pain wrenching from her throat. I hear Michael's heavy footfalls as Grace's cry brings him into the room. It goes on and on, a raw sound of anguish, of soul deep pain until her voice falters and she breathes the word, "Michael."

None of us need to ask what she's seeing now.

I glance over at Michael, and his face is grey as he watches Grace relive Lucifer's fall. Grace may be the one trapped in a memory, but Michael is hearing every cracked bone and seeing every spray of blood.

Abruptly Grace tenses up, her teeth gritting and every muscle locking as though she's bracing herself for impact.

Lucifer strokes her hair, rocking her still form. The low hum of Lucifer's voice is a language I don't understand, but I recognize the foreign cadence.

Enochian.

Lucifer's voice is hoarse as though he was the one screaming in agony moments ago, and I wonder when he last spoke in the language of Heaven. I whisper to Michael, still standing frozen beside me, "What's he saying?"

Michael shakes his head without looking at me.

"Come back to me." Lucifer switches back to English before whispering more words in Enochian, flowing from one tongue to the next.

After the Fall was century upon century in Hell, surrounded by the worst of humanity and their own personal torments with nothing but demons for companionship. Grace is lost in a torrent of blood and pain and anger so deep that there was always the risk that she'd be unable to surface.

I'd told her that. I'd almost wanted her to say no.

The three of us wait for what feels like hours as Grace rides out the terrifying depths of Lucifer's psyche. Michael and I give them what little privacy the small house offers, standing sentry at the edge of the room. I'm reluctant to stray any further in case something goes wrong. Because *this* is the spell going right.

"You don't have to watch this." Michael starts as though he's coming out of a trance.

"Yes, I do," he replies.

Grace blinks, taking in a shuddering breath as she wrenches herself free from whatever corner of Hell she's trapped in. "How?" she asks, her voice cracking on the word.

We're all holding our breath, no one more so than Lucifer. Every memory, every action over thousands of years has been laid bare before her. Would she ever look at him the same way again?

Grace swallows thickly before speaking again. "How did you go through all that and come out who you are?" There are tears on her face, and I know I have no business watching this, but I'm rooted to the spot. "How do you love me?"

The devil is dumbstruck as he looks at her, wonder in his eyes. He finds his voice enough to ask, "Are you all right?"

Grace nods. "I need some time to sort it all out, but I'm okay. I'm still me." She leans closer, brushing her lips across Lucifer's. "Nothing has changed."

I want to give them the time and space to soothe their frayed nerves with each other, but the spell will only last so long. We need to do this now or else everything I just put them through is for nothing.

"It worked then." My words snap Grace back to the present and out of the bubble she and Lucifer have ensconced themselves in.

Grace stands up, swaying on her feet for the briefest second before getting her equilibrium back. She rolls her shoulders, forcing the stiffness from them as she feels Lucifer's power flow through her.

"Can you do this?" I ask, abandoning my spot at Michael's side to stand in front of Grace, scrutinizing her for lingering weakness. "You need to be at 100% or it's too risky."

"I'm fine." There's no trace of waver in her voice, no signs that she was mentally flayed a few minutes ago. "It's all a bit raw, but nothing I can't handle," Grace says, squeezing Lucifer's hand. I hate the pang of jealousy that surges in me at their united front.

"Let's do this."

I CLIMB into the passenger's seat of Grace's car. She sits behind the wheel, staring blankly through the windshield.

Lucifer and Michael took off ahead of us to give Grace some breathing room.

She turns on the car, the air conditioner sputtering for a moment before coming to life, but makes no move to drive.

"The way he sees me—" Grace stops herself, leaning her forehead against the hot leather of the steering wheel as she closes her eyes, and I'm glad Lucifer gave her the space to process. She obviously needs it.

"There was so much darkness. So much hate and betrayal, and he was so alone." Grace swipes at her eyes, before turning to me. "But in those last few moments where I was so lost everything started getting brighter. It was so bright it almost hurt. It was like staring into the sun, and in those last seconds before I woke up I realized that it was *me*."

Grace puts the car in gear without another word, and we drive on in silence.

THE MANSION LOOMS AHEAD, the stately columns and manicured plants hiding the nightmare within. This side of town is quieter than the tourist centers. Only a few cars drive sedately down the street, and the sidewalks aren't choked with gawkers. It's the perfect place to hide in plain sight.

Grace parks the car a block down the street. Lucifer and Michael are already standing at the edge of the property, eyeing the gate warily.

"She thought of everything," Lucifer says. "The wards are even on the roof."

I hadn't held much hope for an aerial assault, but the idea of even more protections to break through is disheartening.

Lucifer wraps his fingers around the iron fence. Michael and I immediately rush forward to stop him. "Don't touch it—"

Lucifer cuts me off with a look as he twists the iron until it snaps. The wards poured into the metal bind the soul, but those at least are nothing to Lucifer. A rush of icy air blows past us with a hiss as Lucifer sends the soul plummeting down to Hell where it belongs.

He takes a step back, letting go of the fence. It's nothing more than a physical barrier now, just decorative iron that holds no match to any of us. "One down."

I glance past the decorative spires of the fence to where the wards shimmer in the air. One down, and still so many left to go.

I hand Grace a Hell-forged knife, the blade as long as my hand and wickedly sharp. Weapons feel more than useless, but I can't stomach the idea of Grace walking in unarmed.

"Stab first, ask questions later," I direct. Grace takes the knife, testing the weight in her hand before tucking the sheathed blade into the back of her jeans.

"Elissa."

I turn around to see Michael, and I can't pretend I didn't expect this. He shifts from foot to foot, filled with the same battle-ready nervous energy that flows through all of us.

This isn't the time or the place. I need to focus on finding Caila and not getting anyone killed, not on my love life, but I can still hear the low hum of Lucifer's voice, whispering to Grace in a language I'll never understand. I can still see Michael's stricken face as he watched it all, and whatever embers of hate and anger I still hold for him sputter and die.

Two thousand years is long enough to hold a grudge.

"I was wrong all those years ago." The words spill out of Michael as he rushes to get them out before I go inside.

Just in case one of us doesn't make it out.

"I did the wrong things for the right reasons, but that doesn't make it any better," he confesses, clasping his hands together as he tips his head back, gazing up at the unfeeling blue of the sky. "Heaven was going to kill you, and there's nothing I could have done to stop it. I did what was needed to save you, and I won't apologize for that." Michael lets out a long exhale as he forces himself to look at me, and there's so much regret in his eyes. "I still love you. I never stopped."

Michael's words fade into nothing, blocked out by the sudden ringing in my ears.

I'm reeling.

Heaven did this.

Heaven stole our life together, our happiness.

I see Lucifer and Grace in my peripheral vision, more casualties of Heaven's hypocrisy and rules. They survived Heaven's meddling once, but not without their own sets of scars.

I stare through Michael, seeing nothing but the gate, the wards, what I have to do, and I almost wish she had picked another angel.

Somewhere deep in my memories I still hear the sound of the water lapping against slick stones and smell the acrid scents of cheap wine and human filth rolling off my father as his head slips beneath the waves. And once again that same realization strikes me.

If she had picked another angel, I'd walk away and leave her to it.

"Elissa?" I blink, the deep blue of Michael's eyes coming back into focus, his brow furrowed with worry at my silence.

They say your life flashes before your eyes before you die. I'm not dying, but it all comes pouring back in that one moment, washing over me like the flood.

Michael standing stiff-backed in the corner of my study and the look of utter bafflement on his face when he realizes I can see him, like a child being surprised that closing their eyes doesn't grant them invisibility.

That first kiss, my back against the stone wall with his

hands in my hair, hands that had wielded blades and could tear down cities that still tremble the slightest bit when they touch me.

Days and nights lost in skin and touch, in tangled bedsheets and torn robes, all our earlier hesitance forgotten when need takes hold.

The dead look in his eyes when he tells me I can never understand his duty to Heaven.

So much time and so many mistakes.

"You have terrible timing," I murmur as I grasp the collar of Michael's shirt and yank him downward, pressing my lips against his. This isn't goodbye. It's not one last kiss before dying.

Year after year of longing pours into that kiss. Michael's hands slide around my waist, pulling me against him, and I don't need a bond or shared memories to know that he understands. This kiss is a promise that we don't die today.

Heaven doesn't get to win, but neither does she.

We do.

I extricate myself from Michael's arms and blast through the first ward.

INSIDE THE GATE the air is oppressive, the weight of the magic surrounding us pressing down on our bodies, squeezing the air from our lungs until even breathing hurts. Grace looks over her shoulder at where Lucifer stands just beyond the mystical barrier, his shoulders a tense line as he watches us.

The wards are a Gordian knot that would take days to entirely unravel. Layer upon layer of spells shimmer in the air, far more than were visible from the outside, and I'm at a loss for where to start. Brute force worked for the first, but most of the spells surrounding us won't go down easily. The magic is powerful enough to be almost sentient, and unmaking these spells will be like cutting the wires on a bomb. One wrong move could turn the air to acid or boil our blood in our veins.

She knows we're here. The second we crossed the gate she felt it, so I can only imagine that she's watching us for her own amusement from some secret lair like a comic book villain.

Grace stays close, hovering only a step behind me but this time I don't argue or ask for space. Every extraneous movement is another chance for a single wrong step to end us. The angelic wards are the closest to the house, but getting to them requires us to wade through the tangled mire of everything else first.

I hold my hand up, and Grace freezes. The air shifts, the threads of the spell glowing bright gold. We're close enough that it's readying itself to trigger. "Don't step any closer. This one is basically a mine," I say.

Grace blinks. "Like a landmine?"

I nod, already focusing on untwisting the strands of the spell, murmuring the incantations that will dissipate the power. It pulses an even brighter gold, enticing me to take another step closer the warm glow. I rock on my feet, my weight shifting forward and I almost take the step, the thrall so subtle that I don't even notice until the light brightens to the point where it's almost painful to look at.

I shake my head, shifting my weight back onto my heels and away from that step that will rip as apart with all the finesse of a claymore mine, and I feel the flood of indignant rage press against me from all sides as the spell fights to do what it was made for.

The pressure grows, and I hear Grace gasp beside me, but I can't spare her any attention. Deep in the twisted mess of gold I see a strand just a bit darker than the others and I blindly reach back, grabbing Grace's arm and drawing on her borrowed power to snap that thread.

A high-pitched whine tears through the air around us as the spell melts away. My eardrums are still ringing when I take a tentative step forward, testing the ground. When we aren't immediately blown up I continue forward with Grace right behind.

We inch closer to the house, eyes wide as we scan our surroundings for more traps. And there are always more traps. Removing all the spells enrobing this house is an utter impossibility, so we tunnel through only those that are in our path to the door and the angelic wards wrapped around it.

I'm drenched in sweat by the time I reach the steps of the porch, the effort of tearing down the spells dizzying even with siphoning power off Grace. I put my foot on the first step, and Grace yanks me backward, shoving me to the ground as a stream of red flame arcs through the air like a whip. It's close enough that I can feel the fabric of my shirt smolder for an instant, and it would have ripped both of us apart.

"Thanks."

"Don't mention it," Grace replies as we mount the steps tensely, waiting for another attack.

Nothing.

Looming in front of us are a dozen wards like what was hidden in Caila's bedroom, along with more spells to blind Heaven to this house's very presence. Grace offers me her hand, but I shake my head. "Lucifer's an angel. That borrowed power won't work on these."

These sigils hang in the air, black and heavy, looking like tears through the sky. Slashing through these is going to be a lot more difficult that pulling down plaster and drywall in Caila's bedroom. They're all entangled in each other, so there's no hope of taking them down one at a time.

I need to rip them down all at once, hopefully without killing myself in the process.

I plant my feet, staring up at the sigils, the oily black lines oozing through the air like a poison. I summon up every reserve of energy I have and a few that have long since run empty. I close my eyes and see Caila chained and broken, Michael bleeding out in the backseat of a sedan, and Lucifer clutching Grace as she loses herself in his darkest memories.

We've all been through enough.

I open my eyes, and the wards burn.

12
MICHAEL

The wait is excruciating.

I've never been one to sit on the sidelines and watch the battle go by without me. Even when my heart was miles away from the front lines and I felt nothing but the heaviness of my blade chipping away the parts of myself I still recognized, I never thought to ask another to fight in my stead. Yet here I am, watching frozen as Elissa and Grace pick their way through the twisted viper's nest of spells, holding my breath when they trip a ward or Elissa falters in her casting.

Elissa's shoulders are stooped, and her pace has slowed to crawl by the time they reach the house, exhaustion written over every inch of her frame. Magic at this level is draining in the best of scenarios, but diffusing spell after spell while remaining on high alert for another attack would be too much for anyone. Even with Grace and Lucifer's combined powers acting as a battery to sustain her, I can see her strength dwindling. It's only the force of her will keeping her upright at this point.

And I'm trapped outside the gate, helpless.

Lucifer paces like a caged animal, his eyes never leaving Grace as she follows in Elissa's footsteps. A whip formed from flames cuts through the air in front of them, and it's Grace's quick reflexes that save them this time. Lucifer goes still, wrapping his hands around the broken fence, and I hear the iron creak beneath his grip. I've never been one for wanton destruction, but I can see the appeal of ripping something apart right now.

Instead, we watch and wait.

Elissa steps onto the porch alone, leaving Grace waiting at the bottom of the steps. Her back is to us as she faces the sigils, the thick mass of lines and curves pulsating in the air like a living thing.

She's so drained already that despite all my faith in her abilities I don't know if she'll be able to succeed at all, or what the cost might be to her even if she does.

It happens all at once. A sonic boom tears through the air, loud enough that even my ears ring and a few car alarms on the street start blaring. One by one, the blackness of the sigils erupts into white hot flames, spreading from one to the next before winking out of existence altogether.

I expect Elissa to turn around looking triumphant, but she staggers on her feet for a moment before crumpling to the ground.

The barrier holding us back is gone, and Lucifer and I rush inside, picking our way along the cleared path as fast as we dare.

Grace kneels beside Elissa when we arrive, her hands clasping Elissa's limp fingers, her brow furrowed in concentration as she pushes whatever dregs of strength left between the two of them into Elissa. Her fingers twitch under Grace's touch and Elissa startles herself awake a few breathless moments later, sitting up quickly enough that she winces as her head swims.

She blinks a few times, scanning the empty porch as she looks for anything else we might have missed before dragging herself to her feet.

"Are you all right?" I ask, unable to hide my concern. She looks spent, as though she's been awake for days. Deep purple shadows have carved themselves under her eyes, but I know we have no choice but to keep going.

"I'm fine." We all hear the lie, but Elissa's already squaring her shoulders and pushing aside fatigue and pain. "I don't like this," she mutters. "It's all too easy."

"That was easy?" Grace can't keep the incredulity out of her voice.

"We're all alive. No one's bleeding." Elissa takes a step closer to the door but hesitates as though waiting for yet another trap to spring. "Way too easy."

The front door is flanked by two bromeliads, the spiky red blooms looking like a festive version of a medieval weapon. "I take it we're going in through the front door?" Lucifer asks, "It's not like your entrance was particularly subtle. We're not surprising anyone."

Elissa sighs but nods and Lucifer twists the knob. Unlocked. After all why bother with something as mundane and human as a deadbolt when you have this much power cloaking you?

The door opens silently, revealing the impeccably decorated hallway. A rug in shades of pale green and cream cuts through the dark wood of the spotless floors. An enormous vase of white flowers overflows from the thin console table just inside the door, the heady scents of gardenia and rose wafting from the vase. An ornate chandelier above us casts a bright glow of refracted rainbows from the beads of gold and crystal that dangle down.

"Are you sure we didn't just break into Martha Stewart's vacation home?" Grace asks.

Elissa chuckles, but her amusement cuts off quickly when the walking corpses appear.

They emerge from the doorway at the end of the hall, shambling along the plush rug. They're in varying stages of decay, some with fresh blood still sticky on their skin, others missing eyes or limbs, others already so decayed that their bones creak and rattle with each step.

"Can't you do something?" Grace backs up slowly, running into Lucifer at the rear of our group.

He steadies her, squeezing her shoulders reassuringly but shakes his head. "Their souls are long gone. They're nothing more than walking meat."

The closest of the corpses looks like she was a nurse before taking a bullet to the face. Medical scrubs covered in dried gore cling to her greying flesh. Half her cheekbone is missing, her one brown eye remaining gazes vacantly from beneath a mane of stringy brown hair and dried brain matter. She grabs for Elissa, her movements too slow and easily telegraphed to be a real threat.

Elissa jumps back, and Lucifer takes her place, lopping the woman's head off with his blade before either of us can react. The head thumps to the floor, leaving a streak of decomposing flesh along the immaculate rug.

But the corpse keeps coming.

The headless body continues to stagger forward. Lucifer kicks at her femur, and there's no missing the brittle crack as the bone snaps. She pitches forward onto the ground but still keeps coming, dragging herself by her hands and pulling the shattered leg behind.

More and more of them pour out of the adjoining doors, the sheer crush of bodies overwhelming in the tight space. I have my own blade in my hands, hacking and slashing blindly. Lucifer is at my back, beating back the creatures that have crept around in an attempt to flank us, and for the briefest instant it's glorious, the adrenaline of fighting at my brother's side blocking out the fear.

Elissa and Grace hug the wall, their own weapons at the ready, but none of the creatures even look at them. Instead, they swarm Lucifer and me, forcing us apart.

"Go," Lucifer yells, gesturing to the staircase.

"Do you honestly think I'm leaving you two to the zombie hordes?" Elissa snaps, jamming her blade into the neck of the remnants of a man wearing a business suit and missing both eyes. Her knife sticks, the blade caught on a collarbone and she kicks him in the chest with one booted foot until he goes down, freeing her knife.

Lucifer is losing ground, the dozen or so corpses surrounding him shove him through an open door into another room. I elbow one in the neck and slice the throat of another, the leathery skin flapping open as its head lolls backwards. My foot crosses the threshold and the heavy oak door slams shut, trapping us both inside.

Etched into the wood of the door are the increasingly familiar lines of the angel weakening sigil.

I tug on the doorknob, already knowing that it won't work. It's fastened tight, held shut by magic.

"The Hell with this," Lucifer snarls, pushing me aside. Lucifer presses his palm against the door, but the expected Hellfire doesn't come. He kicks the door, but it barely rattles on the hinge.

"Don't bother," I lean against the wall, straining to hear anything through the heavy wood and plaster. "The wards were just a decoy. She wants us out of the way, and we played right into it."

13

ELISSA

The heavy double doors slam, cutting us off from Lucifer and Michael, and everything freezes.

The zombies back off immediately, staggering away through the other open doorways without giving us a second look. As soon as the last walking corpse disappears down the hallway, Grace and I practically sprint to the door.

"Don't touch it," I order, crouching down to inspect the handle. "You can't trust anything in this house." I hover my hand over the ornately carved silver handle and feel the whisper of magic curled around it. Sighing, I duck my head. Of course. Why would anything be easy?

"Lucifer? Michael?" I call.

"Are you two all right?" Lucifer's muffled voice is barely audible through the screen of magic and the thick layer of oak.

"We're fine," Grace replies. "The zombies backed off as soon as the door shut."

"The door's warded from the outside." I lean as close to the door as I dare, straining to hear them both. "I'm not even sure what it is, but it's nasty. I can try to get through it, but-"

"Don't risk it," Michael interrupts, and I relax just a bit more at the sound of his voice. "Don't worry about us, just watch yourselves."

Walking away from them feels like a terrible decision, but it's the only choice we have. Grace and I turn away from the door and head deeper into the house, feeling like every clichéd horror movie heroine deciding that the best option is to split up and cover more ground.

At least no one said, "I'll be right back."

The sense of wrongness builds with every step, a thick dread that catches in the back of your throat like a sickness. Every inch of the house is decorated in flowers or golden filigree, a Victorian level of absurd opulence with the juxtaposition of death in the air that makes my skin crawl even more.

A vacant warehouse or a crumbling cabin would make sense. China cabinets and gold-lacquered mirrors don't.

For all that she suffered during the spell to strengthen their bond, I envy Grace. Lucifer's presence wraps around her like a balm, a comforting reminder to each of them that the other is still breathing.

I don't have that protection, and I already feel like every nerve is stripped raw after casting spell after spell. It's like I'm still caught in the blood memory that lead me here, the heavy scent of decay lingering in the air that no amount of flowers can cover up.

Grace doesn't comment, but I know she senses that soul-deep rot as well.

I could have chosen this path. If Lucifer hadn't come to me, I might have chosen this in my search for power and buried myself so deeply in vengeance and corruption that no light could reach me again.

This could have been me.

And Caila is here – kind, loving Caila who devoted her eternity to protecting those who needed it most. Not for vengeance or anger or even a misguided sense of guilt. Because it was the right thing to do.

We pause at the foot of the curved staircase, the emerald green of the carpet directing us upward just like an arrow. The zombies are gone, leaving nothing behind but the few hacked off limbs littering the foyer, and there's nowhere to go but up.

The stairs are silent, the thick pile of the carpet muffling our footfalls, and Grace and I keep to the center of the stairs, avoiding the banisters out of pure habit. At the top of the stairs are several rooms with heavy wooden doors, closed and no doubt locked, but at the end of this hallway the largest hangs open, the dazzling rays of the afternoon sun streaming through.

I glance at Grace, and she nods, taking a step forward until she's beside me instead of a few steps behind.

Whatever's coming, we face it as equals.

We walk through the door into another room straight out of a high-end home décor magazine. Except I've never noticed iron chains bolted to the floor gracing the pages of Town and Country.

"Elissa. Grace. I've been waiting."

I barely notice the small brunette that speaks. I only see Caila. A heavy iron chain is fastened to the collar around her neck, every link etched with spells and sigils. When she hears our names, her head snaps up, a look of pure alarm flashing across her dirt and blood streaked face.

Another figure is chained a few feet away, this one male. His arms are wrapped around his knees as though he's trying to make himself as small as possible. He looks up for a moment and I hear Grace gasp the name, "Phenex."

Phenex. I squint my eyes, trying to reconcile this dirty, broken creature with the beautiful angel that followed Lucifer's steps. His clothes are little more than rags, the once-white suit stained with blood and filth and pock-marked with slits and holes.

What has she been doing to them?

"Now that we've all made our intros, I have a proposal for you both."

I take a deep breath, summoning every shred of restraint I've ever had to keep from launching myself at this woman. . . this creature and tearing her apart.

She's lounging between the two chained angels on a chair that can only be described as a throne, high-backed and white except for the golden lion's paws holding it up, it's as ostentatious as everything else in this house. Her legs are slung over the chair's arm, the white silk of her pants flowing over a pair of nude patent pumps with blood red soles.

"Oh Elissa," she tuts, the haughty tone of her voice infuriating familiar. "Don't tell me you don't remember me." She climbs to her feet with an ease borne of centuries of pampered living, and I look beyond the uptown pretension, beyond the Louboutins and the impeccably styled chestnut brown of her hair to remember powdered wigs and corsets and yards of impractical lace.

"Brielle?"

"Glad to see you still remember some things."

Versailles
1683

Oh yes, I remember.

The Sun King is at the height of his power, and his glittering palace of Versailles has barely been completed for a season when I first lay eyes on Brielle Carrette.

The first seeds of the revelation have already been sewn

when the glorious structure rose up, casting its golden shadow on the starving peasants, but the time of reckoning and guillotines is still years in the future, and the elite still wield their power without discrimination, seeking endless increases to their wealth and influence.

And none are so pious as to bar a witch from a place in their court provided that witch is beautiful and talented enough to earn her seat at the table.

We three more than met those criteria.

Brielle is the daughter of a minor country lord who hungers for more and finds it in Roux Baptiste. The wildness that drips from the two of them like so many jewels proves intoxicating to the members of the court already bored with the decadent excesses of their small lives. Even buried under powdered wigs and with their skin painted the color of fine porcelain, there is no mistaking those two for just another pair of striking nobles.

Scraps of rumors about a comely young witch and her even more powerful lover have been filtering down to me for the better part of a year. I haven't been searching for them, but I'm far from unaware of who and what they are when our paths finally cross.

Any who can claim a drop of noble blood make the pilgrimage to Versailles to curry favor and gaze upon the majesty that the ego of Louis le Grand has wrought, and even I am not immune to the draw of that spectacle.

Nor am I immune to the charms of Brielle and Roux.

What Brielle lacks in discretion or breeding she more than makes up for in beauty, and it's the talk of the court that winter how her father allows her to gallivant across the country unchaperoned and unmarried.

Roux is not the marrying type.

In those early days, no one knew where he came from or who his family was. He snatched the name Baptiste from the air, claiming it as his own with the same rashness that lead him to claim Brielle.

But the first moment I lay eyes upon them, I know that Roux isn't just another witch. He's something much more powerful and much more terrifying.

Nephilim.

The angelic offshoots are as varied as humans in their personalities and their abilities, but they all have one thing in common.

Short lifespans.

Some are strong as a dozen men, some see visions of the future, some can heal or kill with a touch. But no matter what powers their Heavenly parentage might have bestowed upon them, they never have long in this world before Heaven finds them and cuts them down like a dog in the streets.

Roux is already living on borrowed time, and he knows it, so he uses those stolen days to live as he wishes. I can find no fault in that, even if his methods are less than orthodox.

Roux cannot lift oxen over his head, nor does he have visions of the future. His touch can incite desire as any handsome man's can, but he doesn't hold life and death in his uncalloused palms.

But his voice? His voice can remake the world in whatever image he wishes.

It takes only a whisper of suggestion from Roux's lips and the words become a worm tunneling into the quarry's brain, subverting their will and replacing it with Roux's own.

My first true sense of his power came a scant few weeks before our first encounter. Roux had selected a viscount, nearly at random, and with a few honeyed words convinced the man that he was a long forgotten bastard son. The viscount had the misfortune to have bred three daughters but not a single boy, and suddenly Roux found himself in possession of a bloodline and an ancient ancestral home.

And just like that the whispers about Brielle's behavior were abruptly silenced. Lack of propriety never seemed to matter much as long as the right name is attached to the sins.

I wasn't blind to the danger of the games they played. Brielle shucked off her innocence at the first chance, and I could hardly blame her for wanting to be free of the stifling world she was born into. And once Roux set his eyes on her, decorum and obedience gave way to mutual obsession.

And when they chose to make room in their little circle for me, it was intoxicating and impossible to resist.

Brielle's charms went many miles beyond a pretty face and pleasing company. She learned to read fortunes at the feet of her family's servants, awakening abilities long dormant in her bloodline.

The women who scoured the stone floors and cooked the meals taught the pretty dark-eyed child how to pry the future from bones and shells and wisps of smoke, filling her ears with memories of Barbados, of freedom in a land without the bitter cold.

I never learn their names, those servant women who risked violence and abuse to mold Brielle's young mind to their liking, but I can't help admiring them, even if they were the ones that put her on the path to darkness. Stolen away from their homes and their lives, it seems only fitting that they steal their captor's daughter away from the life he imagined for her.

And when Roux caught Brielle's scent, there was no turning back.

I meet them the first time at a soiree after one of the tedious court dinners. The unmarried girls preening themselves as they search for a wealthy husband have been sent to bed in the care of their hawk-eyed mothers, leaving the men, the harlots, and the lucky widows to sip brandy and play cards.

Snow falls outside the palace, adding another layer to the thick blanket of white coating the countryside. Tiny chunks of ice cling to the hem of my petticoats, weighing the heavy lace of my skirts down even more.

Laughter rings out like a bell as I enter the drawing room, and when I scan the crowd for the source, there they are. A few strands of Roux's russet hair peek out from beneath the powdered wig, but I don't need to know his name or see that unusual hair to know him. Even seated his height is apparent, and when he stands as one of the women leaves the table, the other men look like children beside him. The power flows around him, so strong the air shimmers like the stone of the roads in the summer heat, and it's like looking at Michael again, uncanny and still so beautiful.

There is no mistaking Roux for anything but something *other*.

His slate blue eyes flick up from his cards and meet mine. His mouth curls into a wide smile, his teeth a white slash through the pink of his full lips. Without breaking my gaze he leans closer to Brielle and speaks loud enough for me to hear from across the room, "I believe the one you saw is finally here."

Brielle rises from her seat and strides across the room toward me, the satin of her emerald green gown rustling with each measured step. One her age rarely wears such dark colors. Even I clothe myself in light blues and shades of silver to hide my own otherness in plain sight.

Not Brielle. A walnut sized emerald rests in the hollow of her throat, the same stone I saw around the wrinkled neck of a dowager countess a few weeks past. No doubt the old woman would declare it a gift if asked, but I know better.

She stares at me as though appraising the value of a new gemstone she wishes to acquire or a prized racehorse she's considering betting on. The tendrils of her mind press against mine as her dark eyes rake across my body, and I almost mentally bat her away out of pure reflex.

Almost.

Something about them both intrigues me even though every instinct screams at me to keep my distance from their madness. I've barely spent five minutes in their presence, and they have both proven that the word discretion is not in their vocabulary. Already whisperings in the church from as far as Rouen speak of their exploits across the countryside.

Heaven has no place for half-breeds, and if God's servants here on Earth are beginning to question him it will only be a matter of time until the angels take notice and come down to mete out their own idea of justice.

And yet, I still sit down beside them and pick up my own hand of cards, tossing a fistful of silver coins into the growing pile of wagers.

"I'm Elissa."

Roux bares those white teeth in a smile again, and I think of wolves and tigers, beasts that show their teeth as a reminder that their clenched jaws are just waiting for the chance to close around the next yielding throat.

"We know."

Brielle laughs again, the sound high and free like the breaking of glass, and I know how dangerous the forces they're toying with are. I know that it's not a matter of *if* Heaven finds them, but *when*.

But then Roux presses a glass of brandy into my hand and Brielle whispers to me in that musical voice unbroken by loss and deprivation that "we can learn so much from each other." I toss my cards down onto the table, barely noticing the bad hand as Brielle leans closer, the heady scent of roses floating around her and adds, "You and I will be like sisters. I've seen it!"

Underneath the powder caking her skin is the flush of

youth and the maddening excitement of freedom. Her eyes linger on Roux, and he feels her gaze. Without looking, he slides his cards from one hand to the other, twining the fingers on his free hand with Brielle's before pulling her closer and kissing each delicate knuckle.

She's so young, her heart still so breakable, and when Heaven takes him from her, she'll be alone.

A witch alone and shattered can do terrible things.

"I'd very much like to hear more about what you've seen," I say, and Brielle beams. I wonder if I ever carried such trust in my heart.

For one golden year, I did.

I don't need the sight to see Brielle barreling heedlessly down the same path I trod so many years ago, but perhaps I can keep history from repeating itself.

WINTER STILL CLINGS to the land with its corpse-cold fingers when the angels come for Roux.

Two months have passed since that midwinter eve when I met them both, and since that night the three of us have been thick as thieves. Slowly but surely my guard has dropped away, and the wild and careless pair have clawed their way into my affections.

That all ends one night with the scent of fire and the screams of horses.

I'm ripped from sleep by the sound of frantic voices echoing through the darkened inn, and when I throw back the heavy velvet curtains the grounds are lit as bright as day, the sky orange with fire. Roux and Brielle are missing, and I don't need to see wings to know that the angels have found us.

I barely pause to grab a shawl to wrap around the thin shift I wear. The icy March wind cuts through me but I barely feel it as I follow the trail of blood through the snow, away from the inn to where the burning stable lights the night skies.

The sharp crisp scent that has always whispered Heaven to me cuts through the scents of smoke and the scorched fur from the dying beasts trapped in the barn, and I rush towards the blaze. With each step closer the snow melts more under my feet, soaking through my thin slippers, my skin already numb.

Under the frantic shrieks of the dying horses I hear Brielle screaming, "Get back!"

The doorway looks like the gate to Hell the clergy so loves to speak of, but I don't hesitate as I rush towards it. I'm close enough that the heat singes the edge of my shawl when two arms yank me backward, nearly pulling me off my feet.

"You can't save them, madam!" the innkeeper yells as he drags my struggling form away from the fire. More and more of the snow melts into a slick mire of mud as men rush with buckets of water from the half-frozen well to toss uselessly into the blaze.

I struggle free, striking him with an elbow and twisting away from his well-meaning grip, but I barely make it two steps before the roof caves in and Brielle's voice is abruptly silenced.

I drop to my knees in the mud, filth soaking through the white cloth of my shift. The men rush around me as they fight the desperate battle to beat back the flames before the wind can carry a stray ember to the roof of the inn.

Somewhere underneath it all, I hear wings.

"You died," I blurt out, and a crumpled copy of a smile crosses Brielle's face at my words.

"Did I now?"

Her accent is different, centuries away from her homeland dimming the French, but the cadence is still the same. The wigs and corsets are gone, traded for a sleek blowout and white silk, but underneath it all it's still her. Even the decorations make sense. Brielle always did hate the cold, so she found somewhere warm to build her own private Versailles. She even gave herself a throne.

And something in the back of my mind whispers, *never trust a survivor until you find out just what they did to stay alive.*

"You died," I repeat, taking a step closer.

Brielle tosses her hair back over her shoulder with the same defiance she showed centuries ago. "Roux taught me many things before Heaven slaughtered him, and so did you. Obviously, I didn't die in that stable."

Her fingers tighten on Caila's chain, yanking her upward. Caila lets out a pained yelp as the collar cuts into her throat, and it's only Grace's hand gripping my arm that keeps me from ripping the chain from Brielle's hand.

"Imagine my surprise when I discover you call one of them your friend," she spits. She grabs the other chain from where it pools on the floor, dragging Phenex closer. He stumbles as he tries to rise to his feet, keeping his eyes downcast.

Even from a few feet away he looks so much worse than Caila. His wings drag on the ground behind him, one hanging at an awkward angle, the delicate bones obviously snapped, and the downy white feathers are broken and twisted and as filthy as the rest of his body. The charred odor of brimstone hangs in the air, almost blocking out the clean ozone scent of angel.

"He's Fallen." Grace's voice rings out. "He's not one of Heaven's."

Brielle chuckles, wrapping a few more links of Phenex's chain around her hand and tugging him closer. He nearly falls again but manages to shuffle forward. She reaches her hand up to brush his matted hair off his forehead, and he flinches violently. "I'm well aware," Brielle coos, gripping his chin in her thumb and forefinger and forcing his head up. His sky blue eyes gaze blankly at nothing.

"This broken little phoenix had the terrible luck of being in the wrong place." She drops the chain and Phenex staggers backward, pressing himself into the corner again, the trembling of his slim frame visible from across the room.

Brielle continues as though nothing happened. "He fought me quite a bit in the beginning, so I had to teach him his place. It took a few decades, but I'm nothing if not patient."

No. No, she can't have.

"Decades?" Grace sputters. "I saw him two weeks ago."

"I do forget how very human you still are," Brielle sniffs, but doesn't elaborate.

I feel ice pouring into my veins, colder than kneeling in the snow that day. Colder than riding away from the inn alone and burying Brielle's stolen jewels by the road, whispering apologies to the frozen dirt because I certainly wasn't going waste breath on prayers.

I mourned her. I mourned them both and cursed Heaven until the icy wind stole the breath from my lungs.

Heaven wronged her, but this. . . she couldn't have done this.

"You opened a door." She dips her head in a quick bow, looking so proud of herself I want to scream, but instead I hiss, "Are you insane?"

"Oh Elissa, we're all mad here."

Grace tenses next to me, but I keep my eyes on Brielle's smug face when I speak. "Time flows differently in Hell. A few hours here is a year there. It's the same in Heaven." I can't keep the tightness from my voice when I continue. "And she made a door."

Brielle drops Caila's chain, the heavy links clattering on the floor, and Caila is crawling across the floor to Phenex's side as quickly as she's able. He whimpers when she says his name. I hear snatches of the musical lilt of Enochian, but the rest of the room seems forgotten as Caila tries to soothe the shattered angel.

"They've gotten quite cozy. It's almost cute. Or it would be if I didn't know what their kind was capable of." Brielle turns back to me. "I didn't make a door, dearest Elissa. More like my own private suite."

"But Phenex was in Hell," Grace interrupts. I want to tell her to be silent. To turn and run from this room while she still can, but I can only watch and listen as Brielle answers her.

"He was in Hell, yes, but not *his* Hell. It took him years to stop begging for Lucifer to save him." Brielle settles herself back on the white chair, looking as calm as if we were just two old friends sitting down for tea. "And the other one? She barely lasted a week before she kneeled. And now that you two are here, we're finally ready."

My mind races, and I search for an escape. The spells and sigils are carved into each link of the chains and end to end on the collars, leaving no weak spots to exploit. Even if Grace and I could escape unscathed, we'd have to leave Caila and Phenex behind and there's no way that's happening.

Caila's soft voice filters back to me as she strokes Phenex's dirty hair. The blond fallen angel resided in Hell for millennia, taking his place as Lucifer's right hand. I'd heard all the rumors. It was a spot earned by fondness and familiarity and not by skill as a torturer, but none dared to question Lucifer for his choice of head lieutenant.

To break a Fallen so thoroughly. . . what torments had

Brielle subjected him to? She had to have heaped more and more anguish upon him for years, for *decades* to reduce him to this shattered creature trembling in Caila's arms.

She made a door, and now it's unguarded.

"You cannot be seriously thinking you can claw into Heaven as easily as you tunneled into Hell," I challenge, hoping Brielle's arrogance will force her to keep talking and give me the time to think.

She sighs, rolling her eyes as though being forced to explain herself to a child. "Of course I don't think these two will be enough for me to tear through the gates." Brielle glances disdainfully over at Phenex and Caila, her nose wrinkling at the state they're both in even though her manicured fingers were what caused it. "But they will give me enough power to take those two delightful treats you brought me."

Brielle smiles, and I wonder how I missed seeing the seeds of this in her years ago. I'd spent all my worry for how she might suffer after Roux's death. She had seemed so young, so in love and so very breakable, but I'd been so wrong.

Brielle Carrette was never fragile like a flower.

She was fragile like a bomb, and all of Heaven, Hell, and Earth falls in the blast zone.

"Two Archangels," she continues. "Hell will bleed, and Heaven will kneel, and they will regret the day they touched him."

"I won't let you do this." It's an empty threat, and we both know it, but it still has the desired effect of incensing Brielle.

"You're going to fight for the angels then?" she spits, standing up from her throne and stalking to window where the first rays of the sunset have dyed the skies the same flame-red of Roux's hair. She turns her back on us like we're nothing to gaze out at the sunset.

"That's rich coming from the one who dreamed of watching Heaven burn. You hate them as much as I do. The

Elissa I knew doesn't forget, and she certainly doesn't forgive." Brielle turns away from the glass, her entire attention focusing on Grace. "And you! Heaven ripped apart your family, and you take one of them to your bed?"

"And I killed the angel that did it," Grace snaps. It's easy to forget that hidden beneath the golden curls and the pretty dresses is a spine of pure iron. Grace looked the Archangel that murdered her family in the face and ended him. She doesn't need me or Lucifer shielding her.

"All of Heaven and Hell knows just what you did to Uriel," Brielle replies, stalking towards us. "All that power wasted though." She shakes her head. "Raziel was the one who held the sword. It took me nearly ten years after Roux but it was worth the wait." She presses her lacquered pink lips together at the memory. "It took so many bargains, but one day the demons brought him to me, and I knew what I was going to do with him."

She doubles back to where the angels crouch and she grabs Caila, twisting her fingers in the tangled mane of the angel's pale hair. The knife slides out of her sleeve, blackened metal, thin as a fireplace poker but wickedly sharp.

Forged in Hell.

She draws the blade across Caila's cheek, but she doesn't react as a bright streak of blood appears along her skin.

"If Heaven takes one of mine, I take one of theirs, but the power, Elissa. It was intoxicating. I know why Roux was too much for the world. I know why the angels had to kill him." The tip of the knife trails down Caila's neck before pausing at the hollow of her throat. Brielle could shove the blade through before I could move.

Brielle looks up at me and smiles. "If humanity felt that power, we would bleed Heaven dry for another taste. But I barely have to lift a finger. I just need to open a few more doors."

"You want to pit Hell against Heaven?" I stammer, barely able to believe she's suggesting this. "You want to start another war."

"The war's already started," she replies. "With both Heaven and Hell's generals locked in my living room until I bleed them dry, it'll be chaos. Roux did always appreciate a good mob. Pity he missed the revolution."

Brielle was always a survivor. She lived through the wrath of Heaven to be reborn through the fire and didn't flinch from selling bits of herself to demons in exchange for the chance to cut down an angel. She could kill us all and sleep peacefully tonight.

And somehow I never noticed that seed of cruelty within her.

I'd been right all those years ago. A witch alone and heartbroken can do terrible things.

"Do you have any idea how many humans are going to be caught in the crossfire?" Grace demands. "You were mortal once, weren't you?"

Brielle rolls her eyes. "I got over that. They're all dead already. They just don't know it yet."

She presses the knife deeper into Caila's throat, and the angel holds her breath, her blue eyes wide as the saucers of those ridiculous teacups she loves so much.

"Please!" I beg, fighting back every urge that tells me to *do something*. "You killed Raziel. Let that be enough!"

Brielle laughs, and it sounds like broken glass. "Raziel was nothing but the sword. A foot solider. Your precious Michael gave the order. It'll be slow for him."

14
MICHAEL

Unsurprisingly Lucifer isn't responding well to being penned in.

A heavy crystal bowl strikes the far wall with enough force to shatter into glittering shards that fall onto the plush rug like icicles. The bricked over windows block out the sunlight, and two of the three lamps in the room have already fallen to Lucifer's temper tantrum, plunging the room into a dim half-light.

I can't blame him for wanting to take this place apart piece by piece. Something about the absurdly perfect curation of this house is infuriating.

But one of us needs to at least feign being calm.

"Are you going to just sit there and do nothing?" Lucifer snaps, hefting a twisted iron fireplace poker in his hand and slamming it into the wall of bricks covering the window. A few crumbles of brick dust scrape away, but beyond that nothing. Trapped in here we're as weak as humans.

"I'm trying to think of a plan," I reply acidly.

"Master strategizer," Lucifer mutters as he stalks away

from the bricks. "Do it faster. Grace is still alive but I'd rather not test it."

"Do you think I want to be stuck in here?" I explode before deflating at the realization that I have no idea what state Elissa might be in. "Brother, I just got her back."

Something flickers in Lucifer's face for an instant before he turns to the wall. The wallpaper is an intricate damask pattern of gilded roses, the metallic paper glinting in the faint glow of the one remaining lamp. Lucifer bashes the fireplace poker through the wall, ripping through the paper and paneling and tearing chunks away bit by bit until he finally exposes a swath of wires and pipes.

Glancing over his shoulder with a smirk, he reaches in and rips out the wires, plunging the room into blackness.

"Happy now?" I grumble as my eyes adjust to the sudden darkness.

"Not yet, but I will be." Lucifer presses the still sparking wires against the wallpaper, watching as the pattern begins to blacken and bubble under the heat, the ink melting until finally the paper catches.

"The wards are in the walls," Lucifer says, his earlier frenzy forgotten as an almost eerie calm descends over him. "There won't be any walls soon enough."

I know I'm gaping at Lucifer, but I can't help myself. My brother always did favor the battering ram approach, but as the smoldering wallpaper starts to catch I can already feel the figurative shackles loosening. The first tendrils of flame eat through paper and adhesive and one by one the hidden sigils inside the walls are consumed.

Lucifer takes a few steps back from the growing blaze and sprawls on one of the frilly armchairs. He props his feet up on the spindly legged coffee table, watching unconcerned as the flames climb the walls, consuming the curtains that decorate the blocked windows. A few sparks fly onto the carpet, and the scent of burning wool joins the room as the threads start to burn.

The heat is oppressive as the fire wreathes the room, the smoke thick as fog, but Lucifer doesn't flinch. He sits silently, every muscle coiled in anticipation of the last ward breaking.

We both sense it the moment the last one falls, and Lucifer springs up. He's a blur of smoke and rage as his foot connects with the door, splintering the half-burned wood outward.

Oxygen rushes inside and the flames flare even brighter as we rush to freedom with a cloud of fire at our backs.

15

ELISSA

The house falls into abrupt silence as the power cuts off.

With the hum of the air conditioner hushed, my own heartbeat rushes to fill the auditory void, pounding in my ears. The faintest hint of smoke tickles my nose, sharp and bracing over the twin scents of flowers and decay. The russet glow of the setting sun filters into the room through the large picture window overlooking the backyard, the orange light carving Brielle into silhouette where she stands, her unflinching hand holding a knife to Caila's throat.

I hate being helpless.

With fists or magic, I know I could best Brielle. She's amassed an incredible amount of power in the last few centuries, hoarding it like a dragon, not caring where it came from or what the cost.

But her powers are borrowed and bought or stolen outright. She can fill her house with walking corpses and siphon off the magical energy of every cemetery in the city, but it will only last for so long.

The dead can't sustain her forever, and she knows it. That's why we're all here.

Brielle presses the blade deeper into Caila's jugular, and a thin stream of blood drips from the cut, pooling in the hollow of her throat. It's not a killing wound by any means, but it's enough to remind me of how quickly that cut could deepen. Brielle moves the knife aside and draws her fingers over the wound, and I see the faint golden glow of her angelic essence pulse for a moment before fading as Brielle steals a bit more from her.

Brielle's eyes slip shut for an instant before she peels them open, her blissed out gaze focusing right back on me, daring me to take a step closer. "This one has so much guilt." My eyes dart back and forth from Caila's stricken face to Brielle.

I want to tell myself that Brielle is crazy, that the loss of Roux and the solitude snapped her mind and drove her to this. I want to blame the spells, the demons she trafficked with, whatever injuries she sustained in that blaze, but that would all be too easy.

I see nothing but the cold calculation of complete sanity in her face. Brielle knows exactly what she's doing, and that makes her words far more terrifying than the pitiable ramblings of the insane.

"I didn't know their kind even understood the word guilt, but I learned a few things in Hell myself." A full-bodied shiver rips through Caila at the word. Behind me, I feel Grace's hand brush the bare skin of my wrist, the growing shadows in the room concealing the contact, and the power that floods me at that brief touch is almost dizzying.

The devil's on his way, and *he is pissed*.

"She whispered the names off like a list to herself each night. There are dozens and dozens, but a few show up the most. Milly. Serafine. Marianne. Will. Uriel. Grace." Grace's head snaps up at the sound of her name, and Brielle notices.

"Oh yes, this pathetic creature is your self-appointed guardian angel. Piss poor job she did though. She failed your grandmother and your mother so completely that they both ended up dead. She's even the reason your father grew up an orphan. Couldn't even save poor, weak little Milly from a human."

Scorn drips from Brielle's voice and the knife presses harder into Caila's skin as her mounting anger makes her grow careless. "That's what angels do, Grace. They ruin everything they touch."

"Roux was half angel," I counter, trying desperately to get her to shift the knife just enough so that I can make my move.

Brielle's lips curl back in a sneer at that, but her reply is cut off by the crack of wood splintering from downstairs and the sudden roar of fire. Lucifer and Michael saunter into the room a moment later, the flames consuming Brielle's palace trailing behind them.

As he strides into the room Lucifer looks every inch the devil we were all warned about. His impeccable suit remains untouched by the smoke and soot, and I know him well enough that he's preening just a bit at the tremor of fear that Brielle can't quite hide before she steadies herself. Lucifer draws out every bit of shock and awe he can muster, the embers of Hell itself glowing in his eyes. Michael is a step behind him, looking every bit God's fiercest warrior with a sword in each hand.

For all the power Caila and Phenex can wield, there's no comparison to the might of an Archangel, let alone two.

Lucifer isn't one to stand in stalemate for long, and when he takes a step closer to Brielle she slashes her wrist across Caila's throat.

Or tries to.

We all forgot Phenex, even Brielle. Broken and beaten,

huddled in the corner as far away from his tormentor as he could get, Phenex watched and waited for his chance.

With her attention focused on Lucifer and the growing roar of the fire to drown out the clink of chains Phenex forces himself to his feet and grabs a fistful of Brielle's dark hair, yanking her backward.

The knife clatters to the floor as Caila pitches forward. Grace and I rush to her but it's Lucifer who catches the weakened angel before she hits the ground, hissing as the enspelled chains brush his hands.

Grace slips her fingers under the collar, searching for a clasp and finding only a keyhole in the front of the heavy iron.

"There's a key," Caila chokes out. "It's around her neck."

"Of course it is," I grumble, standing up and rolling my shoulders.

Now that her hostage is out of reach, I'm ending this.

I spare a glance at Michael, his weapons at the ready, and consider telling him that this is my fight.

Screw that.

Brielle went it alone, and I see what it turned her into.

If I hadn't met Caila and found a reason for my endless existence, I might have one day done the same.

We're all so much stronger together.

Brielle twists in Phenex's grip, fighting to throw him off, and his rusty reflexes aren't fast enough to avoid the conjured flame in her hand. She shoves her burning palm against his cheek, and the smell of scorched flesh adds to the increasing cloud of smoke billowing into the room.

Phenex doesn't even seem to feel it. The tattered remnants of his suit flutter around him like dirty bandages as he darts out of reach. His broken wing drags behind him, but still he circles Brielle, his teeth bared. He looks savage, like the years in Hell at her mercy stripped away the guise of humanity Phenex normally wears as well as those pale suits.

Brielle reaches out both her arms and clenches her hands into tight fists. Already weakened from constant abuse, Phenex goes down first, clawing at his chest in agony. I manage to draw in one more breath before it strikes me.

I feel her hand gripping my heart, feel every delicate finger bone pressing into aortas and arteries, squeezing tighter. My arms drop to my side, feeling more like lead than flesh and blood and bone, and black spots march across my vision like insects.

I fight to stay conscious as she cuts off my arterial blood, the grip growing stronger, and I waver on my feet.

And suddenly I'm not choking on my own blood in a burning room with the smell of scorched carpet and smoldering wallpaper around me.

I'm on the hillside, *my* hillside, back in Sidon, pebbles and dust under my bare feet as I stare out at the ships and wish. I'm so young, so alone and afraid but somewhere between one step and the next I slip into the skin I wear now. I watch masons carve my villa from the rocks. Before my eyes, dust and stones become something beautiful and *mine*.

I look over the edge, staring down at the deep azure of the water, and I feel him against my back. Michael's heart beats with mine, and there's love and tears wrapped up in every pulse. I turn to look at him and his eyes grow darker, blue melting into black, into Lucifer's hate-filled gaze. The look's so familiar to me. I see it in every reflective surface I pass – hurt, betrayal, loss.

But not evil. Not cruelty for its own sake. That's why I've never feared him. Michael severed my heart and snapped Lucifer's wings, and still we both ached to forgive him in the deepest pits of our souls.

The balmy heat of Sidon fades as cold creeps in, and I see

flashes of white and red, of Brielle and Roux, of rabbit fur cloaks and red hair whipping in the wind as the carriage cuts through the snow, the horses foaming as Roux pushes them harder as though he can outrun his fate.

Brielle is by his side like a jewel – haughty and beautiful and so beloved by both of us. I've learned many times over that love can so easily be twisted into a weapon, and Brielle's smile is a knife.

Somewhere buried under the flashes of tangled memories I hear Michael's voice screaming my name. The sharp pain as my knees hit the floor snaps me back to awareness for an instant.

"Now you'll know how I felt!" Brielle shrieks at Michael, and I understand it all.

Roux wasn't evil. Reckless and impulsive to the point of being dangerous, his powers were too much for a mere human to be trusted with. Maybe someone in Heaven saw what he would become if they didn't intervene, or maybe they simply couldn't abide anyone challenging their eternal order.

But he was never evil.

The darkness is closing in again, and I see blood on the snow. I drop to my hands, feeling the heat from the flames creeping into the room around me and with the last wisps of breath in my lungs I wheeze, "Show me."

The glamour wrapped around Brielle wavers for just an instant, our combined magics butting heads, and I see a flash of burned hair and wizened skin and sunken eyes before Brielle wrests control back.

It's enough.

I blink and when my eyes open again a slender blade protrudes from between Brielle's ribs, silver coated in red. Michael wrenches the blade out of her back and she falls.

Suddenly, I can breathe again. I gasp as I draw air back into my lungs, my bruised heart pumping oxygen through my blood again. I hear Phenex coughing a few feet away, the collar still preventing him from healing properly.

Michael's arms are around me, easing me to my feet. His hand pushes my hair away from my clammy face, and the worry in his voice finally cuts through the ringing in my ears.

"-Elissa, it's over. Please, look at me." I tear my eyes away from Brielle's crumpled body to look at Michael, and his face breaks into a smile so filled with relief that I can't help returning it.

"Hey," I murmur, brushing a streak of soot off his cheek. I take a deep breath and immediately regret it as the smoky air brings on a bout of coughing. I stagger away from Michael to where Brielle lays, her blood painting the soft green and gold of the rug a deep burgundy.

The faint gold of a chain half hidden by her hair catches my eye, and I crouch down beside her, plucking the blackened key from where it rests under her shirt. The slender chain snaps easily and the movement pulls Brielle back from the brink of death, her eyes sliding open to stare up at me.

Brielle pulls her lips back, the feral smile baring bloodstained teeth. "You're too late," she whispers. "It's already begun." She slumps back to the ground like a broken doll, her eyes falling shut as I stand up.

I move on autopilot, pressing the key numbly into Grace's hand, watching as her deft fingers unlock the collars from Caila and Phenex. Caila kicks the chains away the instant she's free while Phenex still looks shell-shocked, at though he can't quite believe the weight of the collar is finally gone.

He tries to take a step and his legs nearly give out under him, but Grace is there, offering him a shoulder to lean on. Phenex lifts his hand up, tracing his fingers over the ugly scar marring the skin of his throat before his arm drops limply to his side.

The flames lick up the walls around us, and the doorway is

a complete inferno. There's nowhere to go but out the window.

Lucifer grabs a spindly-legged chair tucked against a white-lacquered writing desk and heaves it through the window, shattering the glass. He grasps Caila's shoulder, pulling her out of the daze she seems still caught in. "Are you strong enough to fly?" he demands. Caila nods, spreading her wings, the tawny gold of her feathers looking shockingly whole compared to the mess of Phenex's.

Lucifer peers over her shoulder at where Grace supports a barely mobile Phenex as he stands frozen, staring blankly into the blaze. "I need you to take Grace," Lucifer says, his voice every bit the commanding general. "He can't fly. I'm not even sure if he can walk."

A deafening crack cuts through the air as half the staircase collapses, and it's becoming increasingly obvious that the rest of the house won't be far behind as the blaze eats through floorboards and support beams. The faint noise of sirens in the distance grows louder as the neighbors finally take notice of the smoke pouring from the windows.

Michael herds me closer to the window as Caila and Grace make their escape. Lucifer gathers Phenex into his arms with a surprising amount of gentleness before taking off himself, and I know we've just added a sixth member to our little band of misfits.

An instant later we're all airborne, the last streaks of sunset hidden as the burning house stands out like a torch against the evening sky. As Michael's wings take us home, the mansion glows like a second sun behind us, but all I see is blood on the snow.

This isn't over.

⚜ 16 ⚜
MICHAEL

Everyone lived.

I think we're all more surprised by that fact than we should be.

Grace's house seems to have become the de facto home base for our motley group of celestial outcasts, and while we're all wrecked in one way or another right now, I feel lighter than I have in centuries.

Once freed from the chains and the toxic magic that bound them, Caila and Phenex's injuries heal swiftly. The superficial wounds and burns that covered both of them have already faded into unmarred skin, but Phenex's crushed wing is another story entirely. He'll be in agony as the fragile flight bones knit back together slowly, and the healing will take days at least, though his blank face doesn't appear to even register the pain.

I try not to think of Lucifer wandering through Hell in those first days, dragging his shattered wings behind him.

The adrenaline hasn't yet given way to exhaustion for any of us. Grace and Caila hover over Phenex, trying in vain to draw him back into some semblance of himself. I watch, feeling useless as Grace draws the curtains in the smaller bedroom, blocking out the glow from the streetlights and turning the room into a cave. Phenex wraps his undamaged wing around his body like a blanket before wedging himself between the bed and the wall as though he's trying to shrink his presence down to nothing.

Lucifer waits just outside the doorway, barely able to look at the state Phenex is in. It's not disgust at his weakness or even the expected rage at what the witch did that holds him back.

It's regret. I've seen that look often enough on my own face.

It's the look of a man seeing his own responsibility for the ruin of someone he cares for.

"This isn't your fault," I offer, though I don't expect Lucifer to be any more accepting of absolution than I ever was.

"No," Lucifer replies, dully. "I didn't force him to fall. I didn't force him to follow me out of Hell. I didn't force him to stay on Earth and end up in that bitch's crosshairs."

Caila's voice filters out of the room as she sings softly, Phenex relaxing visibly at the sweet sound. *"He was a singer, some say a sinner. Rolling the dice, not always a winner. You said he was lucky but Hell he made his own. Not part of the crowd, not feeling alone..."*

"Sinatra," Lucifer murmurs. "He did always like Sinatra."

We've all been stripped raw over the last day, injuries and soul bonds and dredged up memories peeling away our defenses, and it's easy to forget old grudges and betrayals. In daylight, we'll slip back into that familiar armor, but something between all of us has changed permanently.

The word forgiveness lingers in the back of my brain, but I don't dare to believe it just yet.

Grace creeps out of the bedroom, quietly pulling the door

shut behind her. At Lucifer's questioning look she shakes her head. "Give him time. I think he's in there somewhere. He just needs time to realize that it's safe to come out." She takes Lucifer's hand, pulling him closer to her as the weight of the day seems to drain from both of them.

I wait for that familiar stab of envy, but it doesn't come.

Grace turns to me, a tired smile on her lips. "Elissa's outside. We've got this covered. Take her home, Michael. We'll figure things out tomorrow."

Elissa sits on the front porch, staring out at the streetlights. The ginger cat is perched on the porch railing, its tail twitching lazily as it stares down at her.

She doesn't look over her shoulder at the creak of the door opening. She's been expecting this, expecting me.

"What's next?" I ask, sitting down next to her on the stoop. She leans into me, letting the weight of her body rest against my shoulder.

I feel her shrug more than I see it. The yellowed glow of the streetlight casts her face half in shadow, and it would be easy to blame the dark smudges under her eyes on the lightning. She looks resigned, the bone-deep exhaustion that covered her in the mansion fading into quiet acceptance.

"We prepare," she says. "Brielle ripped open a door to Hell, Michael. Maybe more than one." Elissa falls silent as two inebriated young women stumble along the sidewalk, the shorter of the two giggling at something her companion just whispered into her ear. Their laughter echoes in the street long after they've passed, a jarring reminder that the world continues on oblivious.

"Things are going to start bleeding through," Elissa continues. "Souls, demons, who knows what else." She twists on the step, turning to face me fully for the first time. "I don't even entirely believe she's dead. She's a necromancer. You know she had some kind of contingency plan. None of this is over."

I let her words hang in the air. She's right. Everything we went through wasn't an end. It was just a beginning.

"That's not what I meant."

Elissa tenses, holding her own silence for far too long before she speaks. "I won't hold you to promises you made when you thought one of us was going to end up dead."

"What if I want you to?"

One year out of two thousand. Even for her lifespan, the time we spent together was barely a sliver and for me it was far less, but I still remember every day, every minute as the only time I've been truly happy since the first days of creation.

Heaven's meddling and my own fear stole it from us once. I won't allow it to happen again.

WE RETURN to that shotgun house on the wrong side of town, to the living room littered with Caila's broken treasures and Elissa's bare, Spartan bedroom. She unlocks the door, and it takes every ounce of control I bear to keep from pinning her against the wall and taking her breathless on the front porch before the door even closes.

She's here and real. Streaks of ash and dust give her skin the faintest grey pallor, and in the jaundiced light of the street lamps, I can almost believe she's some glorious idol carved from stone, a forbidden wonder meant to seduce me from my duties.

But I've already tossed aside duties and orders.

God's Sword.

God's Fists.

God's Obedient Weapon.

No more.

For the first time since I opened my eyes millennia upon millennia ago when creation was new and I knew no better, my hands are my own. My choices are my own.

Free will. Lucifer was right after all. It just took me quite a bit longer to see it.

Elissa hooks her fingers through my belt loops, tugging me closer to her. The front door gapes open, but she's in no hurry to cross the threshold. Instead she stops in the doorway, releasing her grip on my jeans to wrap her hands around my neck. Her slender fingers stroke the short hair at base of my skull, and she pulls me down to meet her lips. For the first time in too long a kiss between us doesn't feel like a goodbye. It's not an ending. Not this time.

Her lips open under mine, our tongues tasting and exploring under the glow of the porch light. We take a few stumbling steps to the entrance and miss the doorway entirely, but I can't find myself feeling particularly apologetic. Elissa pulls back just enough to utter a hitching breath as I press her against the wall beside the front door.

She curves her leg around my hip, and I catch her knee, hiking it up as the kiss turns harder. This is the Elissa from last night, the wild, wanton creature taking her pleasure without apologies, but somewhere underneath is still the girl from Sidon who believed in forever.

I won't give her reason to doubt again.

We pull apart, our breath harsh already as the slow burn shifts into an inferno. I come to my senses enough to usher us both through the doorway into the darkened house, kicking the door shut as an afterthought. Only a single light glows over the kitchen sink, and it does little more than deepen the shadows, but neither of us make a move to turn on another lamp.

She stops just inside the door, and I step behind her, sweeping the thick mane of her dark hair over her shoulder. I brush my lips against the back of her neck and feel the full-bodied shiver that goes through her.

"Michael," she sighs. Her voice sounds wrecked, as though the armor she shrouds herself in has been torn off piece by piece in the last day until only her bare skin remains.

I know how she feels. It's almost too much already and we've barely touched.

Last night was a fever dream, but tonight is real.

And I want to savor this.

I trail my lips toward her shoulder, tasting the bitter remnants of ash on her skin, a reminder of how close I came to losing her for good.

A little of my control slips as I nip at the juncture where her neck meets her shoulder, and I bite down harder than I intended. Elissa breathes in sharply as the sliver of pain cuts through the haze of pleasure, and she reaches one hand back between us, pulling me closer to press the growing evidence of my desire against her lower back. I bite back a groan, my hands skating up her arms before sliding forward to cup her breasts, and Elissa grinds herself back against me in response.

She never was one to simply lay back and be taken.

My nimble fingers find her peaked nipples through the thin fabric of her tank top, rolling them between my thumb and forefinger as I rock against her squirming hips. Elissa's the one moaning now, and suddenly she's twisting in my embrace, turning so that we're face to face, and my back hits the closed door as her hand fists in the front of my shirt, keeping me close.

As though there was anywhere else I'd want to go.

The scent of pomegranates somehow still clings to her

hair, the lush, ripe scent flitting like a ghost through the ash and smoke around her. Her skin's so warm, every part of her running at a fever pitch. Those long fingers graze the seam of my shirt, her nail catching on each button as she drags her fingertips up my body. Elissa tugs at one button a bit too hard and the threads snap, sending the small black disc flying into the depths of the hallway.

I shrug. "It's Lucifer's. No matter."

She laughs at that, tossing her head back and letting her shoulders quake as the stress of the day bubbles over into hysterical giggles that almost twist themselves into sobs.

She trembles against me, and in a small, cracked voice whispers, "It could have been me."

"No," I state, my flat tone offering no space for denial.

Elissa takes a step back, standing just out of my reach, and when she meets my gaze those pale blue eyes are dry. "I've done things, Michael," she confesses, though there's no trace of the penitent in her voice. "Things I should regret, but I don't." She doesn't elaborate, but she doesn't need to.

I never sought her out, never dogged her steps and gave the cities she visited a wide berth after Paris, but that doesn't mean I didn't keep tabs on her. I could have followed the trail of corpses and grateful women across the country and right to her doorstep.

Sometimes man's justice fails and God's justice is far too slow, and the witch from the cliffs is still there handing out punishment to those that truly deserve it.

Don't hate me for what I can't force myself to regret, her eyes plead.

"If it hadn't been Lucifer, I could have ended up like Brielle." And there it is.

I cut her off before she can continue another step down this path. "That Nephilim's death? I ordered it."

"I know."

"Then you know he hadn't harmed anyone." I sigh, slipping back easily into the memory of the one moment I saw her in our long years apart. I'd let myself be distracted though I hadn't even known the three of them were traveling together. I'd remained in Paris, skulking in alleys like a beggar in the hopes of seeing Elissa once more and sent Raziel and Sariel onward to the countryside.

"I remember them both." The words are true enough. Roux and Brielle were just another assignment. Another set of orders to blindly follow as God's artillery fire, only this shot rippled through the centuries.

"Grifters and thieves with magic and bit of nobility backing them, nothing more. I thought about letting them go, but I had orders," I spit, the word tasting bitter in my mouth. "I was still in Paris while Raziel and Sariel searched the countryside, and they were the ones that found him. Raziel held the sword, but the responsibility was mine."

So many years. So much guilt and regret between both of us.

Enough.

Elissa's hand comes to rest over my heart, and I cover it with my own before letting myself meet her gaze.

"You're not the only one with regrets, Elissa. You're not the only one who's made mistakes," I say, as much for my own benefit as hers. "We can't undo the past. We can only look to the future. Our future."

She and I fit together. We always have, and no witch or angel or even Father himself is going to tear us apart again.

Elissa leans up to kiss me again, but stops just before we touch, her breath ghosting over my lips. "This is real," she says.

It's not a question, but I answer, "Yes" before pressing my lips against hers.

My body buzzes everywhere we touch like electricity

sparking across my skin. There is no point in being coy now, no need to dissemble or hide our desires from each other.

I told myself that I was baffled by Grace's decision to choose my brother over Heaven, trying desperately to convince myself of the folly of choosing Hell and the messy human world over the cold clarity of Heaven. Admitting otherwise would have meant owning up to my mistake.

Metatron forced my hand, but as with Roux's death and all that followed I couldn't lay the responsibly at his feet. It was a far cry from free will, but it was still my decision.

Somehow I know Lucifer will never let me hear the end of this.

Elissa drags me out of my head as she tries to unbutton my shirt, but now that she's within reach again I can't resist peppering kisses across her collarbone, distracting her from her task. Impatience quickly wins out as she pops open my shirt, ripping off even more buttons, the plastic discs pinging on the floor like small pebbles.

Her nails rake across my ribs, and I still can't hide the ticklish twitches of my muscles, but before she can do much more than graze my skin I'm crushing my mouth to hers hard enough that I nearly knock us both off balance.

The bed seems much too far away right now, and I reverse our positions without thinking, pressing Elissa against the smooth surface of the front door. She leans back against the wood, watching me through half-closed eyes. I lift one long leg up, my fingers finding the zipper on the side of her boots by touch. The heavy boot thuds on the floor beside us, and I run my hand up her calf, caressing and kneading the muscle before repeating the process with the other leg.

My hand pauses at the button of her jeans, drawing out the moment, before undoing the metal fastener and easing her zipper down. Her jeans cling to her slim hips as I drag them lower, taking whatever bit of black cotton she wears underneath with them. I slide to my knees on the hardwood floor, lifting one foot and then the other so she can kick the tangle of fabric away.

"Beautiful," I whisper, my voice barely more than a breath, and Elissa's lips curl into that catlike grin I remember from so long ago. I lift one foot up again, tracing my finger along the instep and cursing her just a little for not being the tiniest bit ticklish before drawing her long leg over my shoulder. My lips follow the path upwards, tasting the skin of her calf and knee before stopping at the crease of her thigh, so close to where she wants me.

One of her hands scrabbles for purchase in my hair, threading through the strands, and I smile against her skin.

"Patience," I murmur.

"Tease," she replies, her words melting into a low moan as I dip my tongue into her folds, and it's only the grip of my hand on her waist that holds her upright as her thighs tremble.

She tastes like honey, like the ripe figs we fed each other, the sticky juices dripping over our fingers in the summer heat. She gasps, her hips already rocking against the pressure of my hand.

The smallest gasps and moans escape her under my onslaught, her stomach muscles quivering beneath my hand. Her fingers tighten almost painfully in my hair and she tilts her head back, growling "Oh Hell!" to the ceiling.

I almost have to chuckle. It's too fitting.

My tongue flicks against her slick, warm skin, and the noises torn from her throat are the only chorus of praise I need. Her fingers dig into my scalp, her back arching away from the door as she rises closer to climax, and I lose myself in the taste of her, in the trembling of her legs and her loud, unrestrained cries.

Elissa's hands slip from my head to clench my shoulders as

I push her over the edge, her legs buckling as I never pause in my relentless quest to devour her, the space between her thighs becoming my own Eden.

When the tremors wracking her begin to slow, I kiss my way back up her body, easing her leg back down until she's somewhat standing on her own two feet. When I reach her lips again I feel her smile against me.

"I missed you," she whispers, her voice cracking on the words, and I feel like a sailor on one of the ships she watched from the cliffs. I've been lost at sea for so long that even dry land seems to pitch and rock beneath my feet. She's the shore I searched for, and I'll never stop being starved for her.

"I can't feel my legs," she says breathlessly, and this time it's my turn to wear that self-satisfied grin.

And suddenly we're taking stumbling, half-blind steps down the darkened hallway toward her beckoning bed. I barely notice where we are until the edge of the mattress hits the back of my knees and I end up sprawled on my back with a lapful of Elissa.

This all feels so new.

Elissa shucks her shirt and bra, tossing them over her shoulder into the black void of the room. The curtains gape open from where I left them and the faint glow of the moon filters through the glass. Was it really just this this morning when we were last here?

"You're still wearing entirely too much," she purrs, shoving my unbuttoned shirt off my shoulders as I sit up. She grinds against my hardness, her bare sex pressed against the rough fabric of my jeans, and it's almost too much. I flip her onto her back, reveling in her sharp intake of breath. I toe off my shoes without care, and Elissa's hands are already unbuckling my belt, running steady fingers over the bulge she finds there.

"Tease," I murmur, and she laughs.

"Patience," her lips answer, though there's nothing patient about her actions. She makes quick work of the zipper and then her hands are around my length. My head drops to her shoulder, my groan lost in her hair as she touches me with long, slow strokes, relearning what makes me shudder against her.

She whimpers when I draw away from her long enough to rid myself of my pants, but I'm back in the bed an instant later, all teasing forgotten.

Elissa clutches at me, those ice blue eyes that never left my thoughts boring into me, seeing through every pretense and clawing into the most hidden parts of my soul. I slide my hand around the small of her back, lifting her up and with a hiss of breath I edge inside her.

"Michael," she says my name in a long slow exhale as I fill her, and I feel her body pulse around me like at heartbeat. "Michael," she repeats, the word catching as a gasp in her throat.

There's no space, no cell, no hidden bit of our bodies or souls that isn't tangled together, and I don't need to wonder anymore how Heaven noticed her all those centuries ago.

In this room in the city or another at the edge of the world, she unmakes and rebuilds me with every breath, her nails clawing into my skin as though I'm made from clay, marking me in a way no celestial weapon ever could.

Her hips roll upward, meeting my thrusts in perfect harmony. She's close already, her muscles clenching around me as the pleasure coils within her like a spring. She spirals higher and higher, and neither of us need wings to capture a taste of Heaven anymore.

Elissa arches upward, her spine curving as rapture steals the air from her lungs, and she is undone. The world could be ending around us, the universe crumbling back into the dust it sprang from, and I'd notice nothing but my arms around her, anchoring me to her as I drive into her deeper and finally let go.

Then we're both heaving for breath, aftershocks shuddering through boneless bodies, and I brush my thumb over Elissa's kiss-bitten lips.

I remember every moment with her, every laugh and every sly smile, every touch and even every tear. If I survive until the universe ends, hers will be the last face I see before the stars my brother lit with such care fade to blackness.

We settle into tangled sheets, all too aware that the world still looms outside. Elissa fits herself against my side, tucking her head under my chin as exhaustion finally defeats adrenaline and lust and sleep claims her.

The painting along the back wall is barely more than a square of blackness in the faint moonlight, but I know somewhere in the shadows the storm still rages and the painted waves crash against the rocks. Somehow though, the swirling waters have changed. The sun still hides behind the screen of black clouds but the darkness feels different.

Humans call the might of nature God's wrath, as though the ocean bears grudges and the winds feel envy.

I have been that wrath. I have watched villages burn and held lives in my hands. I have torn wings and snapped bone. I have been a blunt instrument, raining destruction down with no more free will than a hurricane.

I have been God's Poison.

Elissa shifts beside me, her eyes opening to stare up at me in the darkened room. "Rest," she whispers, pulling me down against her.

She molds herself to my side, still smelling of ash and pomegranates, and her fingers slide through mine.

Not His hands. Not anymore.

Before my eyes fall shut, I look up at the darkened square of the painting again. The choppy waves still swirl the sea into a frenzy, threatening to drag the unwary down to the depths, but eventually the sun will tear through those black clouds.

All storms break, and the sky will never seem bluer than in that moment when the clouds part.

17
ELISSA

Somehow in these last few days this ragtag band of celestial rejects has begun to feel like a family - Hell's masters, Heaven's defectors, and humanity's guardians all bound together under the New Orleans sky.

But if you look closer, you'll still see the duct tape and zip ties holding us all together.

Erasing the traces of Brielle from the house is the easiest part. Broken drywall and shards of crockery, torn fabric and burned feathers are all swept away, and thick clouds of sage smoke billow through the corridors, the acrid scent as cleansing as iodine on a wound.

We shove the shredded sofa into the alley for trash day, and a few days later a replacement shows up. Even the darkest days can't dim Caila's enthusiasm for online shopping.

The replacement is upholstered in smoky grey velvet, the shade so much softer than the lurid blue of its predecessor. It's quieter, though Caila can't quite resist adding a few throw pillows in vivid turquoise and mustard yellow, to my great relief. We've had enough changes without my resident angel embracing beige.

The warped metal of the security door? We can blame that on artistic license. The new lock works, after all, so the twisted metal is only harmless decoration and not another grim reminder. And the scorch marks on the desk and floor beneath it? That's just distressed wood.

We're all frayed around the edges, but somehow we're stronger for it.

And across town, where the streetlights get a bit brighter, and flower boxes line the windows instead of bars is our second home.

Grace is the beacon there, Lucifer's light in too many years of darkness, and if she loses her footing in this strange new world of angels and magic and century-old grudges, someone's always there to catch her.

I wondered in those early days after the fire if the glut of shared memories will tear those two apart once adrenaline and fear wears off and the harsh light of reality streams in. I couldn't have been more wrong. The bond between them slips into the background again, the link no longer occupying the forefront of every thought, but instead becoming as unconscious as breathing.

After nearly drowning in Lucifer's history, Grace is finally able to truly comprehend what it means when the man who lit the stars looks at her like she's the sun.

On the surface, Lucifer is unchanged. I won't pretend to know the Devil's innermost thoughts but the way he gazes at her when she's not looking. . . I wonder if anyone in creation has been so loved.

I pity anyone who tries to come between those two.

Phenex still buries himself within a fortress of his own mind, the years of torment making him reluctant to lower his defenses, but both Caila and Lucifer manage to coax moments of lucidity from him. The beautiful angel who loved pleasure and longed for Heaven is still in there somewhere, hidden behind that web of scars and screams, and none of us are willing to give up on him.

Trust has never come easy for Lucifer, yet another reason we got along so well. With thoughts of Heaven's plans for Grace and the rest of us all still swirling through his mind, Lucifer's loath to trust any angel, especially one still ostensibly tied to Heaven. But when Caila's voice crooning an old Sinatra standard is the only sound that quiets Phenex's nightmares old loyalties and grudges are forgotten.

Caila, sweet Caila with her pastel dresses and porcelain teacups has changed most of all. There's no danger of her trading the dainty high heels for biker boots anytime soon, but her survival came at the cost of her innocence. Under Brielle's hands she endured the worst of humanity, and her scars might be hidden but I still see them. They're in the shadows in her eyes and the way her hands twitch at loud noises.

She has always been a fixer. Caila made me care again, after too many centuries lost to numbness and regret. Bit by bit, she's drawing Phenex out of his living nightmare, and restoring him is healing them both.

And then there's Michael. My Archangel.

He and Lucifer tiptoe around each other, and snide comments nearly come to blows daily. Thousands of years of bad blood can't be forgotten in a few days, but I can see the specters of who they both once were when the world was young and they were unbroken.

They're brothers again, and they won't let Heaven steal that a second time.

My Michael.

I think some part of me knew my life would be changed for good that first day back in Sidon. Heaven sent an angel to make sure I wasn't a threat, and doing that made a threat of me.

When night falls and the noises of New Orleans start to fade, I sit on the steps, gazing out into the overgrown grass of the backyard and watch the few stars bright enough to shine through the city lights.

I know we are still watched, still judged by those that ruined us once. "Try and take him from me again," I whisper to the skies. It's a threat. It's a promise.

You're at our door a few days later. A different name, a different history, but still the same story.

The thick foundation around your left eye creases in the heat, letting the vivid purple of the bruise show through. You didn't put much effort into hiding it. The bruise isn't your shame, after all, and you've hidden long enough.

You took a bus from Shreveport, but he still found you. You cut your hair and stayed inside, but he still found you.

You stop for a piece of pie in a diner in Metairie, and the waitress calls you sugar and tells you her name is Tara. The look she gives you isn't pity. It's understanding and familiarity. It's the knowing nod of two veterans meeting far from the front lines. She slides you a slice of peach on the house, and written on the napkin is an address.

"He said I shouldn't keep making him so angry," you spit, wrapping your arms around the blue pillow. "I believed that for so long, but not anymore."

"Not anymore," Caila echoes, resting one gentle hand on your shoulder.

You look up at us both, one eye still so bloodshot and swollen from that last punch but the other is clear, the deep brown of the iris as resolute as the earth under our feet.

You haven't been crying. That time is long past.

That first step never gets easier. For any of us.

But when I walk out the door with a name and an address on my lips, Michael's waiting on the other side.

"Watch your back," he says.

I think of the years spent without him and the cold comfort of solitary freedom.

I climb onto my bike and look over my shoulder to where he still stands by the porch, waiting for my words.

"Do it for me."

I rev my engine and then I'm tearing down Iberville Street to the sound of wings at my back.

ACKNOWLEDGMENTS

To Joe - Thank you for indulging my growing obsession with this universe. It's only going to get crazier when I start on book three! I love you.

To Tarin - Thank you for always being my biggest cheerleader, and always being there to crow over how much we love badass female characters.

To my Mom - Thank you for giving me an amazing example of a strong woman to look up to. Without you, none of this would exist. I miss you.

And most of all, thank you to my readers. Creating this

universe and these characters is incredibly rewarding, and hearing everyone's feedback has been wonderful!

Ava

ABOUT THE AUTHOR

Ava Martell was born on Friday the 13th, but she always believed in making her own luck and writing her own story. She is a firm believer that love really does conquer all, but sometimes you have to take the long way around to get there.

She lives in Austin, Texas with her husband, German Shepherd, and two deeply spoiled cats. Ava loves a good gin and tonic to wind her down or wind her up, depending on the occasion, and the only thing better than a good cocktail is a good story.

If you enjoyed this book, and want to receive information on any new books, sign up for Ava's mailing list here.

Follow Ava on social media

Facebook
Twitter
Tumblr
Instagram

msavamartell@gmail.com

ALSO BY AVA MARTELL

First Man

Throw out the rules.

Let the sparks fly.

And pray for a happily ever after. . .

Adam Edwards drifts in the wide world, searching for his next adventure. When his journey around the globe brings him to America he finds a love he never expects and a loss he can't endure.

Ember Pierson is 18 and counting down the days until graduation frees her from small town life. Everything changes when Adam rolls into town and takes a job teaching high school English, and Ember hatches a plan. . .